Penguin Books
The Bucket Shop

Keith Waterhouse was born in 1929 in Hunslet, Leeds, the youngest of five children. His father was a greengrocer. He left school at fifteen and worked at various jobs, from sweeper-up in a cobbler's shop to undertaker's clerk, before becoming a writer. *There is a Happy Land*, his first novel, was published in 1957, and followed by *Billy Liar* in 1959, *Jubb* in 1963, and *The Bucket Shop* in 1969. Mr Waterhouse is also a journalist, dramatist and screen and television writer. In collaboration with Willis Hall, a friend since childhood, he wrote the stage and screen versions of *Billy Liar*. Keith Waterhouse now lives in London.

Keith Waterhouse

The Bucket Shop

Penguin Books

Penguin Books Ltd, Harmondsworth,
Middlesex, England
Penguin Books Australia Ltd, Ringwood,
Victoria, Australia

First published by Michael Joseph 1968
Published in Penguin Books 1971
Copyright © Keith Waterhouse. 1968

Made and printed in Great Britain by
C. Nicholls & Company Ltd
Set in Linotype Times

1

'Look here, any more of that and there'll be no Mumpkin story tonight.'

'I don't *want* a Mumpkin story,' said Melisande. She was a disappointment to her father. He had wanted her to become a child actress, or even an artist like her mother. Perhaps she could have done the illustrations for *Mumpkin Wood*, the volume in which (if things had been different) he would have collected all the tales of Mumpkin Bear and the forest folk that he had attempted to tell his daughter. But most of the stories had never been told. She seemed to prefer the *Jack and Jill Annual*. She was turning out to be quite an ordinary child.

'And daddy, the whole point is if we don't see Peter Pan tomorrow we won't be able to see it at *all*.'

'I honestly don't see why mummy can't take you.'

'For the tenth time, William, I'm going to the . . .'

'She's going to the *hair*dresser's, daddy.'

'Well, I'm sorry, chum, but we'll have to make it another day. It's completely out of daddy's hands. Daddy's got to go to this meeting tomorrow and that's the end of the matter.' He felt absurd, using the nursery third person to a child who stood nearly five feet tall when she could be persuaded to put her shoulders back. It was a habit which he had never made a note to break.

'Yes, but the whole point is it's swimming on Wednesday and Jennifer's party on Thursday and if we don't go tomorrow we hoop – won't – hoop, hoop, hoop!' Here Melisande began to cry in a manner peculiar to herself. It was a tiresome idiosyncrasy which had developed with the whooping cough. Her parents – apologizing for it to the mothers of Melisande's friends – had hoped that it would have disappeared during recuperation. They had been optimistic.

'Don't start that, Melisande.'

'Hoop!'

'Oh, for God's sake,' said William.

'She does have a point,' put in Poodle. 'William? You did promise.'

'Hoop! Hoop!'

'How can I cure her of saying "The whole point is" when every time she says "The whole point is" you chime in with "She does have a point"?'

'She *does* have a point. And stop shouting. You're frightening her.'

'Stop – hoop – shouting, daddy. You're frightening me!'

'Shut up! Do you hear me? Stop that racket immediately or go to bed!'

'You're – hoop – frightening me!'

'I'm not frightening you at all. You're only saying you're frightened because you've heard mummy say it.'

'And you pro-hoh-hoh-hoh-homissed!'

'Bed.'

'Mummy, he pro-hoh-hoh ...'

'Bed! At once!'

William hated these scenes with his daughter, although he often provoked them. The house was not big enough for him to shut the sound of Melisande's sobbing from his ears and thus from his mind. He called up the stairs: 'I shan't tell you again!' and then went and stared angrily out of the window.

In the street a woman was draping washing on a clothes-line strung from a hook on her wall to a lamp-post twenty feet away, a depressing tableau that seemed to William to be more suited to a Welsh mining village. His house was in Fulham, in a terrace of artisan cottages with the promising name of Tulip Street. A house agent had assured him that the district was becoming fashionable and on this prospect he had paid six thousand pounds for the leasehold and painted the front door lilac. But none of the artisans showed any sign of moving out of the street. The tubbed bay tree which he had put out on the doorstep had been stolen. The walls had been chalked on. The only fashionable element in the street, a colour-blind interior decorator who had enjoyed a short reputation while black and white were in vogue and then gone bankrupt, had moved out during the period of his success. His house remained empty for a while and was then bought by a bricklayer. William made some inquiries about the price and was mortified to discover that on present trends his house was worth fifteen hundred pounds less than he had paid for it.

'I wish you wouldn't upset her like that, William. Do you really have to go to this meeting? And what meeting, anyway?'

'I'm not going to a meeting. I've told you already, I'm going to a sale in Islington.'

'In the evening?'

'Yes, in the evening.'

'Then why didn't you tell her you were going to a sale? Why tell her you were going to a meeting? She'd probably like to go to the sale with you.'

'Yes, she'd say she wanted to go and then she'd stand around looking bored and picking her nose and whining for Coca-Cola.'

'Don't be so hard on her. She's only nine. And you did promise she'd see Peter Pan.'

'She behaves sometimes as if she were four. Do you want a drink?'

'No thank you.'

'Well, I'm having one. Anyway, she saw Peter damn Pan last year and hated it.'

William's wife too was a burden to him. She was not really an artist, although he told everyone that she was, and had never shown any aptitude in that direction beyond the circumstance that she had been a secretary in a wholesale paint company when William first met her. At his insistence she had once half-heartedly gone in for an art-appreciation course at the Victoria and Albert Museum but no good had come of this. She had not filled the house with ceramics and potted plants as he hoped she would, and even the Edwardian glass rolling pin which he brought home one evening had been pushed away in a drawer. William had always hoped for a wife who was a 'character'. In the early days of their marriage he had urged her to wear trousers about the house and had given her her nickname, Poodle, in the hope of investing her with some quality of whimsicality. He had tried to persuade her to smoke cheroots. He now had secret hopes that she would become an alcoholic so that he could boast about her capacity to some people he knew casually. 'My wife wasn't in the pub, by any chance? Was she sober?' But she almost invariably refused a drink.

2

Nor was William really an antique dealer.

He was now thirty-five years old. He had been educated at a small public school and had then taken a short service commission as a pilot officer at an RAF maintenance unit in Shropshire, where he was responsible for a balloon hangar full of obsolescent aircraft fuselages. With this experience, and with the vague idea of learning the antique business, he joined a firm of auctioneers but was asked to deal only with lost property that had been left on trains. Eventually, after six unhappy months with a new advertising agency started by some ex-RAF friends and an even briefer stay on the semi-editorial staff of a small wine magazine, he inherited his mother's furniture and china and opened an antique shop in a modest stretch of the Fulham Road.

William could often recognize Wedgwood when he saw it and he had some books about English furniture, but the finer points of his trade eluded him. His mother's pieces sold quickly, for they were under-priced, but then William made a disastrous deal over some restored Regency dining chairs in three sets of five; thereafter he abandoned legitimate antiques as defined by the British Antique Dealers' Association (which denied him membership) and began to specialize in ephemera such as second-hand fruit machines, enamelled advertisements for Bovril, and relics of the First World War. Poodle, in a mood of irony, once referred to his establishment as 'the Bucket Shop'. Since it stood between a male boutique called Trousers Primarily and a bistro called Naught For Your Comfort, the name seemed appropriate to the neighbourhood and so William adopted it.

One of the Bucket Shop's clients was a photographer named Pringle. He worked for the colour supplements and often rented from William items such as pith helmets or cases of mounted butterflies to illustrate feature articles on the age of Kipling or the death of the English summer. He owed the Bucket Shop a hundred and twenty-five pounds.

'Not that I'm pressing you,' said William. 'It's just that I have a very high turnover and I have a lot of cash to pay out.' Not for the first time he reflected with small symptoms of panic that he had been in business for several years without knowing what 'turnover' really meant.

'I've been meaning to take that up with you,' said Pringle. 'It's not that I don't have the money, I can give you a cheque now if you like, but have you ever heard of Desmond Higgins?'

'No.'

'If you ever went to the theatre you would have done. He wrote this marvellous play out at Hammersmith last year.'

'I think I read about it.'

'You didn't read about it because it didn't get reviewed. It's called *Lost*, though we're going to change the title, and it's all about this character trying to wheedle himself into this house as this old lady's son. Whereas for reasons of her own she's trying to pass herself off as his mother. She's blind, by the way, or will be in our version.'

'I didn't know you were concerned with the theatre.'

'I'm concerned with anything that makes money and this,' said Pringle impressively, 'is going to make a bomb.'

William had brought up Pringle's debts not with any hope of getting paid but to prepare the ground for a favour he intended to ask. It was clear to him that he was about to be invited to take part in a business venture; he reasoned that if he were to show interest in Pringle's proposition then Pringle, if only out of courtesy, would have to show an equivalent interest in his.

'It sounds fascinating,' he said encouragingly.

'It's a fascinating play. Higgins has got this idea that it's all about a search for identity or some such bollocks, but in fact if you take out about twenty-five pages of crap, and it's too long anyway, it's a marvellous commercial comedy. Edith Evans. Robert Morley. Ralph Richardson.'

'They were in it, were they?'

'No, you silly sod, it's only been done at *Hammersmith*. Not even Hammersmith – a theatre club in Barons Court. But we need someone like them in it. Sybil Thorndike. Ustinov.'

'He's very good,' opined William.

'Now. They're capitalizing at fifteen thousand pounds in units of two-fifty, and each unit attracts one per cent of the producer's profit. Now if you'd had one per cent of that piece at the Haymarket, you'd have raked in twelve hundred quid by now, and that's only for openers.'

'Four – let me see – nearly five hundred per cent profit,' said William, as if his mental calculus were constantly in use.

'Then there's film rights, American rights, foreign rights – all that's pure bunce. What you can bank on, if the thing clicks, is about fifty pounds a month clear profit on an investment of two-fifty.'

'And you're asking me to . . .?'

'I owe you one-two-five. I don't think it's as much as that but call it one-two-five. So. I can get in on this deal for £500, or two per cent of the show. Now if I raise £375 and you chuck in another £125, cash, that'll give us both a £250 share – do you follow me? – or one per cent apiece. Fifty a month in exchange for one-two-five cash – that's fair, isn't it? And incidentally if you're worried about the old lady being blind, it's all going to be done in sickeningly good taste.'

The figures swirled in William's head, floating, settling, dividing and multiplying like snowflakes under a microscope.

'It sounds fascinating,' he said again. He was not now trying to humour Pringle but was genuinely interested. He had heard of people who had made fortunes out of commercial television and so forth, just by being on hand at the right time and by recognizing business potential when they saw it.

At the same time he did not want to sound gullible.

'What if it flops?'

'What if *My Fair Lady* had flopped?' said Pringle. 'What if anything flops? You take a risk. Anyway, you don't have to decide now. Do you know Kemble's?'

'No.'

'It's a club. Theatrical place, actors and layabouts, just off Shaftesbury Avenue. I'll give you the address. There's a sort of launching party on Monday night, just to get the thing off the ground. You can meet the author, meet the producer, and then you can decide for yourself.'

'Fine,' said William.

'Great,' said Pringle.

'Great,' echoed William.

He had been meaning to ask his favour ever since Pringle started to get into debt with the Bucket Shop. He was no longer sure whether Pringle was under an obligation to him, or he to Pringle, but he thought he would try his luck.

William was having what he would have liked the people who knew him to describe as an affair. It was with a journalist called Rosemary who had wandered into the Bucket Shop one day attracted by a framed Mucha poster of Sarah Bernhardt which William had bought as an original. Pringle happened to be present, borrowing some money. He did not know Rosemary although he recognized her from some Fleet Street pub or other; he scraped acquaintance with her and established that he had once drunk a pint of beer with her husband.

'She's available,' he said to William as she went out of the shop.

'How do you know?'

'I'm telling you.'

Pringle boasted that concerning women a certain reflex action of his was as infallible as the water diviner's twig. William believed him. When Rosemary came back a few afternoons later to pick up an old Suffragette banner which she had reserved, William contrived to be on the point of locking up the shop. He walked along Fulham Road with her and bought her coffee, and he had now been seeing her regularly for over a year.

It was true, he quickly discovered, that Rosemary was 'available'. But availability of premises was another question. They were both married and had nowhere to go, except for public houses where they sat for hours at a time, speculating lasciviously about hotels, somewhere in the Soho area, that were reputed to let rooms for the evening and no questions asked. Rosemary kept urging him to borrow a friend's flat, but there was no one he knew well enough to make that kind of suggestion. He had thought for a long time that he ought to enter into a purely financial arrangement with some incurious bachelor who needed money.

'I'm thinking of just once or twice a week, in the evening. Say between seven and nine. No weekends. And of course we'd leave the place as we found it. You wouldn't even know we'd been there.'

'It depends on who "we" is, doesn't it?' said Pringle. 'It's not this Rosemary bird, is it?'

'No, someone else.' William's answer could have been discreet or boastful: he was not sure which himself.

'Because there's trouble there, if you ask me.'

'What trouble?'

'Neurotic,' said Pringle cryptically. 'In any case I don't like lending the flat out much. I've done it before and it's the kind of thing that works very well on paper.'

'What I had in mind was that we could come to some arrangement. I was thinking if you were agreeable I could split the rent with you. Either I could pay you in cash, by the week, or you could deduct it from what you owe me.'

'If this *Lost* scheme comes off I won't owe you anything, will I? Let me have a think about it. One snag is that my landlady's always buggering about the place. If you did use the flat you'd have to look somehow as if you were visiting me.'

'If it's going to be as tricky as that . . .'

'Another snag, from your point of view not mine, is the rent. I'm paying nine pounds a week there, complete daylight robbery, so that'd run your share up to four-ten a week which is probably more than you want to pay for a quick up-and-down on my bed-settee.'

Several aspects of this conversation unsettled William. He thought Pringle's imagery offensive; it disturbed him to hear

Rosemary classed as a neurotic, for he trusted Pringle's instincts; he was nervous about the prospect of an inquisitive landlady; his idea of an 'arrangement' had not run higher than two pounds a week.

'Let me have a think about it,' he said, forgetting that Pringle had said that first.

'There shouldn't be any snags,' said Pringle.

William felt as if he had devised an ingenious man-trap and then taken three paces back and jumped into it himself.

3

Trousers Primarily was run by two homosexual brothers who were reputed to have brought new dimensions to the crime of incest. Poodle had dropped in to buy the boys' jeans that William insisted on his daughter Melisande wearing at weekends, Pringle to take photographs of the brothers in exchange for some shirts.

'Don't I know you?'

'I think I've seen you in my husband's shop, next door.'

'I know this sounds a bit – what?' said Pringle. 'But if a more or less total stranger said he wanted to photograph your feet, would you *a*, smash his face in, or *b* . . .'

'I don't take a very good photograph,' said Poodle. 'I think I'm not photogenic or something.'

'Not you. Your feet. You have very beautiful feet.'

'They're too big.'

'They're not too big, they're gorgeous. I'm doing some highly boring pictures on the shoe-shop business, all about the take-over thing, and I want a long line of gorgeous feet. Let me give you a card and then you can have a think about it and give me a ring.'

'Watch him, dear, he's all go,' said one of the homosexual brothers. But Pringle had stumbled across the beautiful feet approach very early in his career, during an assignment for a shoe trades magazine. It never failed him.

'At a sale in Islington. Where are *you* supposed to be?'

'Coming back from Wolverhampton,' said Rosemary. 'The last train doesn't get in until 12.44 so I can say it was late and be free till about half-past one, if you like. There's just a chance that Robin might go to the station to meet me but it's a risk we'll have to take.'

Rosemary worked on an expensive magazine and had the scope to pretend to her husband that she travelled about the country more than she did. He was a journalist like herself and so didn't expect to see too much of her. What she didn't mention to William was that her husband was on duty tonight until two a.m. She understood William very well and liked to indulge his sense of insecurity.

'All that's a bit late for me,' said William. 'In fact I told Poodle I'd be home about eight.'

'That only gives us two hours. What shall we do – go to the pub?'

'Failing any other ideas.'

'I've plenty of ideas,' said Rosemary. 'But nowhere to put them into practise. No news of Bristol, I suppose?'

William, with a rashness that now astonished him, had promised to take Rosemary on a weekend to Bristol, the furthest point from London which he felt it reasonable to visit. He could always justify the trip by picking up some Bristol glass which, next to Wedgwood, was easiest to recognize.

Certainly he had to take Rosemary somewhere, for in twelve months their affair had reached consummation only three and a half times. They had not made love at all in the first six months. They had talked about it, kissed in telephone boxes, touched each other in dark shop doorways, promised that next time, next time they would find a place to go. Once Rosemary handed him an erotic letter which he read under a street-lamp and then tore up before going home to a restless sleep. A few nights later, when neither of them could sit still on the hard chairs of a pub called The Goat In Boots, Rosemary professed to make a telephone call and then led him to a flat in Kensington belonging, so she said, to a friend. William fretted because he sensed that all was not as it seemed, but with a six-months record of abstinence behind him he was reluctant to plead impotence on the grounds of anxiety. He forced himself to make love to Rosemary and it was only afterwards, when they lay half-naked on a rug and she began to make smirking remarks about making sure not to leave his trousers behind, that he questioned her closely and learned that this was her own flat but he was not to worry as her husband was on late shift. William was dressed and out in the street in under a minute.

In the summer they went to Epping Forest and made love there, but William was distracted by keepers and peeping toms who might have been behind bushes, and it was not wholly a success. They began to make love one night under a tree in Hyde Park, but were interrupted by boys. Finally, at Rosemary's insistence, William produced the keys to the Bucket Shop and was more or less raped on a pile of Aubrey Beardsley prints under the counter. But the shop was only round the corner from Tulip Street, Rosemary made a loud noise like someone under an anaesthetic, and policemen often tried the door of the shop and shone their torches through the window. William refused to repeat this dangerous experiment.

The Bristol expedition was to be the reward, the culmination and the fruit of several months' self denial. He would tell Poodle that he was going to some sales down there; Rosemary would tell her husband that she was going on a magazine assignment. They would arrive independently and have separate rooms. They would rendezvous at a restaurant chosen by William beforehand from the Good Food Guide, and there they would exchange room numbers. They would return to the hotel separately, but later, when there was no traffic in the corridors, William would come to Rosemary's room or she to his. There would be a security lock on the door to prevent intrusion by chambermaids. William would return to his room, or Rosemary to hers, at about one a.m. in case there had been any telephone calls from London.

But the more William thought about this plan the less

fool-proof he felt it to be. He worried a great deal about house detectives and about the outside chance of meeting someone he knew in the hotel breakfast room. Whenever Rosemary mentioned Bristol he found some excuse for not being able to leave the shop.

'Although there *is* something. I don't want to raise any false hopes but I think I know a man who might lend us his flat occasionally. It's a bit of a risk and I want to sound him out a little more but there's just a chance that it might be all right.'

'When would this be?' asked Rosemary.

'I was thinking probably some time next week.'

'Not tonight?'

'You knew there wasn't much hope for tonight, Rosemary.'

'But couldn't you call him, just on the off-chance?'

'I happen to know that he's out.'

'I see.'

At times like this, when she was disappointed or simulating disappointment, Rosemary would let her mouth droop, lower her heavy-lidded eyes and stare sullenly at her fingernails. When next she spoke it would be to deliver something cutting, spiteful, provocative or distressing.

'Well, you've always got Poodle to go back to, haven't you?'

'You know I never make love to Poodle when I've been with you.'

This was a fiction that William had thought it intelligent to invent at the beginning of his affair with Rosemary. At the same time, on sauce-for-the-goose principles, he tried to create the impression that he was broad-minded and accommodating about her own marriage – he did not relish the prospect of Rosemary making scenes over his wife, turning up at his home or making abusive telephone calls.

But Rosemary did not necessarily accept everything William said at its face value. She divined early on that he was a source of deep, untapped veins of jealousy.

'Robin wanted to make love to me again this morning but I wouldn't. In case you were able to find somewhere for us to go this evening.'

She registered the sinking of William's heart as accurately as if she had him strapped in some cardiac apparatus.

'What do you mean – "again"?'

'I mean after he'd made love to me already.'

'I thought he only made love to you at weekends?'

'I told you that because it's true. But very occasionally he seems to want me at other times, and I am his wife, after all. I did stop him, though. I told him I had to get up to catch my train to Wolverhampton.'

'After he'd made love to you once already.'

'Twice, actually,' said Rosemary. She gave him a smile, altering its constituency from smugness to triumph and then, so that he would not think badly of her, to generous compassion. She wanted to keep William. She had discovered that she had a talent for making somebody really unhappy and it gave her a profound sense of fulfilment.

5

'*What* party?'

'Just a *party*.'

'Then why can't I go?'

'I didn't say you couldn't go, I said you wouldn't want to go.'

'I might like it.'

'Then for God's sake we'll both go. I only mention again that it's a purely business thing and it's not even a party in the sense of the word. It's a business drink with some actors. They want me to invest in a show, which I'm not going to do, and I want them to buy some theatrical prints, which I hope they will.'

'And wives aren't invited?'

'How on earth do I know? They don't *have* wives, half these people.'

'Am I invited or not?'

'For goodness. . . . No!'

'Then why didn't you say so in the first place?'

6

Poodle was ready for an affair. She had been married for ten
years and thought she was entitled to one. She had always been
a faithful wife, not on principle or for reasons of devotion,
but because she had not until lately been thrown into the
company of people who might have offered to vary that status.
She sometimes asked herself (and couldn't answer the question) whether she had always wanted an affair or whether her
interest in having one had developed, by some mutation of the
law of supply and demand, to meet increasing opportunity.

She was not completely sure that William was faithful to
her. To Poodle's mind he was of a naturally shifty disposition,
usually inclined to glide off into another room when a direct
question was asked of him; it was difficult to judge, when he
came in late, whether he looked distraught or guilty or only
tired. Poodle thought his excuses for missing dinner were often
a shade elaborate, especially when he felt obliged to produce
off-handed documentary proof in the way of sales catalogues,
receipts, handbills advertising auctions, and even bus tickets.
But she was not disposed to check up on his movements, in
case her small suspicions were groundless. In the absence of
an affair of her own Poodle was sometimes vicariously ex-
cited by the pretence that William's appetites were so prodi-
gal that he had to seek supplementary relief.

Poodle's life had so far not been momentous. She was an
only child, an orphan: her father, an insurance assessor, died
abruptly after his firm began to investigate allegations of
bribe-taking; her mother was killed in a car-crash while returning home from a country club with a shadowy friend
known to Poodle as Uncle Ned; Poodle, at the age of three,
was put in the care of an aunt. The promise of this adventurous beginning was not substantiated. The aunt was a gentle
vegetarian and her home was a semi-detached bungalow in St
Albans. Poodle was brought up to speak nicely and to take
shorthand at a hundred and twenty words per minute. There
were high-school scholarships and coffee-bar romances, then

an important picnic at which Poodle had her first taste of salami and was seduced by an art teacher. She came to London and worked as a receptionist-secretary, sharing a flat with three girls whom she met through an advertisement in the *Evening Standard*. These became her friends. She had a brief platonic relationship with the brother of one of them, terminating with his emigration to New Zealand; then a broken engagement with an advertising man. Poodle thought later that both of them must have been homosexuals.

She could not remember meeting William. He had the impression that they had been introduced by mutual friends at the sandwich bar of a pub in Earl's Court; but at other times he had a nagging idea, and so did Poodle, that they had met at somebody's party. They married because their friends accepted that they would. They lived in various flats and then when William's mother died they bought the house in Tulip Street.

Poodle was until then content, defining contentment as the absence of any irritant. The move to Fulham and the improvement in William's status from semi-clerk to self-employed antique dealer unsettled her. Although she had no interest in the Bucket Shop and shared few of William's illusions about its possibilities she found that his independence gave her a status of her own. She met people whose horizons went beyond the office or the home, such as the effeminate brothers who ran Trousers Primarily. They gossiped about friends of theirs, women who lived with men, men who lived with women, girls who 'slept around' – the occurrence was too commonplace for them to mention it except by way of additional colouring matter to some scabrous anecdote, but it was on these peripheral morsels that Poodle fed her curiosity. Girls shopping in the supermarket talked matter-of-factedly about their lovers. Mothers at Melisande's school spoke of their au pair girls becoming pregnant, and some of them hinted obliquely at their own adventures. Even William (to camouflage his own activities) sometimes came home with a tit-bit of scandal – a stallholder in the Portobello market might be living with an American student, or someone had told him about a famous actress being someone's mistress. All this had the effect of pornography on Poodle's expanding mind. And one day she ran across one of the girls from her flat-sharing days. The last Poodle had seen of her she was about to marry one of the young men who used to drift in and out of the flat for a meal or to get out of the rain; now she was living quite openly with a film cutter whose wife could not be bothered to divorce him.

Poodle began to feel cheated. William had fetched her into territory in which moral values were excitingly fluid, but he had offered her no incentive to maintain the standards of her own environment. He had done little to adjust her to her new surroundings beyond trying to get her to wear trousers and urging her to collect pre-war comic postcards. He had no eccentric friends who might drop in late with a bottle of cheap wine and probably spend the night on the sofa because their girl-friends had left them. He did not engage her in shrieking, jealous quarrels about other men, or other women. For all his aspirations William had not changed since his days in the basement office of the wine magazine. He wore the same clothes, talked in the same way and made love in the same way, although less frequently. Poodle had now concluded that her life with William was essentially suburban. He had brought her physically to Fulham and spiritually to the fringe of Chelsea, but sexually she remained in St Albans.

'Could I speak to Mr Pringle, please?'
'I think he's out. Would you like to leave a message?'
'Just tell him the girl with the feet rang, would you?'
'The what?'
'Feet. He'll understand.'
'Can't you just leave a name? I'm his landlady, not his personal secretary.'
'It's all right. I'll ring again later.'

7

Pringle's party did not amuse William, for the reason that it did not take place. The basement theatrical club called Kemble's seemed to exist mainly to dispense whisky and toasted sandwiches to the cast of *Apart From That, Mrs Lincoln, How Did You Like The Play?*, a successful American musical at the Palace Theatre. William arrived in Soho shortly after the curtain had gone down on this production and was more or less thrown down the stairs of the club by an eager influx of Negro dancers.

Kemble's was small and wreathed with black smoke from a hamburger steak which had recently been on fire. William's first observation was of a vast number of outstretched hands holding glasses as if for a fervently loyal toast. Through watering eyes he then saw that all the hands were directed towards the tiny bar where the proprietor was trying to satisfy a clamour for drinks.

A girl carrying plates of food high above her head slithered nimbly between banks of corduroy and denim like a grass snake negotiating a rockery. Less adroit, the club's members made their way to the lavatory or to the fruit machine by using each other as rungs on a horizontal ladder, each transit person taking the arms of a neighbour and swinging himself towards another. William, wedged against the banister, found himself used several times in this fashion. Everyone in the room seemed to be laughing, but at different things and thus at a different pitch, so that his ears were assailed by a stereophonic medley of cackles, shrieks and guffaws. There was no sign of Pringle, and William was sure that whatever the stampede of Americans was celebrating it was not the launching of a play about problems of identity that had once been done in Barons Court. The producing consortium of *Lost*, if any were present, had made no effort to engage a corner of the club for themselves. Twice William bellowed at shifting, random faces: 'Do you know where I can find Mr Pringle?' The first man shrugged. The second yelled back: 'Where did you have him last?'

There were a few English people present, evident by their dyspeptic complexions; it struck William that they might be members of the *Lost* contingent who had decided to integrate themselves with the larger numbers of American actors and dancers. One man, with a beard, could conceivably have been the author of *Lost*; another, wearing dark glasses, might have been the director. William tried to look receptive, inviting conversation: thus occasionally someone, squeezing past on the way to the lavatory, spoke directly or indirectly to him. An American said: *'Jesus.'* The Englishman with the beard, probably thinking he knew William from somewhere, paused to belch and said: 'What about that shit at the Royal Court on Sunday?'

'I didn't see it,' confessed William.

'It was shit.'

Each of these constricted encounters resulted in a number of garments being dislodged from the banister rail, which was used as a cloakroom. William, in his cramped position at the foot of the stairs, felt constrained to pick them up. As he tugged at an apparently congealed collection of sweaters and raincoats on the floor a buckled patent-leather shoe narrowly missed his knuckles and an English voice said:

'I'm so sorry.'

'I'm so sorry,' repeated William automatically. He looked up to confront an obscurely recognizable face of which the outstanding feature was a huge mouth shiny with lipstick. William, running quickly through a haze of television programmes, finally identified it with a commercial for cat-food. The girl was holding a cigarette which with a gesture she invited William to light for her. She had been on her way to the telephone but was held up by a sudden shift in the body of people around her, a kind of landslide resulting from one of the members near the bar having moved two full steps backwards to laugh at a joke.

William, who did not have any matches, said again, 'I'm so sorry.'

'You're looking all forlorn and left out of it. Are you with the show?'

'After a fashion.' He crooked his right arm so that he could be observed to be holding his glass in the recognized cocktail party position; recollecting that he had no glass to hold, however, he made a gesture of brushing his lapel and placed his hand in his pocket. 'I'm one of the investors. Or at least . . .'

The large red mouth had formed itself into a wind-tunnel of amazement.

'You must be *stinking* with the stuff. Do you keep it in the bank or under the bed?'

Another shuddering movement by the tightly-packed body of drinkers pinned William against the banister and separated him from his fellow-guest. This time the shift was caused by the entry of several late-comers from *Apart From That, Mrs Lincoln*, who were greeted with shouts of derision from their friends as they tumbled down the stairs. Pringle followed in their wake. As he caught sight of William he cradled his face between his elbows in a gesture of mock fright. By way of apology he shouted accusingly:

'I tried to ring you! You were engaged!'

'I gather your party's been slightly out-numbered.'

'It was such a bloody madhouse here, we've all been sitting in the Trattoria next door. Didn't anyone tell you? Robbie, you sod!' Pringle called with ineffectual reproach to the club proprietor who, with a bottle of wine between his knees, was exclaiming *'Fuck! Shit!'* as he tried to extract the cork.

'*Lost*. Big news,' announced Pringle. '. . . I suppose no one's given you a drink, by the way? I'm going to resign from this place . . . but look, something very exciting's come up. We've been offered a six-weeks tour and touch wood an almost definite offer of a West End theatre.'

'And that's good, is it?'

'It's not good, it's fantastic. Do you know how long you have to wait for a theatre normally? We're having the most amazing *luck*. But. Drawbacks. The big snag is, we've got to put all the money up by tomorrow morning, cash on the nail. Let me get you a drink.'

To substantiate this offer Pringle stood on tiptoe and craned his neck to peer idly over the heads of the drinkers. Having thus fulfilled his obligations as host he returned to William. In this fraction of time, however, the proprietor's efforts with the wine bottle had caused another convulsion among his members, and Pringle found himself facing the girl with the large red mouth.

'Aren't you going to say hello to me, Pringle?' She pressed her lips into the shape of a full-grown carnation to receive a kiss that was not forthcoming. 'Your little friend and I have been chatting, but we haven't actually been introduced.'

'Piss off, darling,' said Pringle.

Unabashed, the girl turned to William. 'I was in New York four years ago. In *The Student Prince*? You know? That very camp revival?' Unaccountably, she seemed suddenly to have acquired an American accent. Even to William it seemed that she was overdoing the interrogative inflection.

'I've never been there,' he said politely.

'How come you're involved with *Apart*?'

'A part of what?'

'The show. *Apart From That Mrs Lincoln*. I thought you were a backer.'

'For Christ's sake,' murmured Pringle.

'Oh, I see,' said William. 'No. I'm involved with Pringle's show. A play called *Lost*.'

The girl opened her wide mouth in a prolonged, soundless scream of laughter.

'And I thought I'd picked a millionaire! Oh dear oh dear oh dear!' A slow croaking coming up from the throat synchronized a sound effect with the animation of the open, quivering mouth, from which now issued a series of high, piercing shrieks. Pringle took the opportunity of planting himself between her and William.

'Yes, well if you don't mind, we've got some business to talk.'

He took William's elbows and, propelling him in the manner of a fork-lift truck, directed him towards the bar. The screeching laughter pursued them and then melted into the general babble.

'Who was that?' asked William.

'Jackie Douglas. Popularly known as the human pillar box.'

'She does have rather a large mouth, doesn't she?'

'I wasn't talking about her mouth. Robbie, *can* we have a drink? We've only been here forty minutes.'

The proprietor was listening to an offensive joke about the Pope, told to him by one of the Negro actors. A flicker of hate came into his eyes but he made no further acknowledgement that Pringle had spoken.

'Robbie?'

'*. . . on-a da can right now, why-a don't you call-a back?*' So the second cardinal . . .'

'Robbie'

The bar was littered with abandoned or half-finished drinks. Pringle took the nearest two – a reasonably full Scotch and what seemed to be a vodka or gin and tonic – and gave William his choice.

'Getting back to *Lost*, it's a question of put up or shut up, because this character we're in with's had too much experience of productions going down the drain when the backers turned out to be non-existent. Cheers. *Christ*, it's got ginger in it.' Pringle grimaced, exchanged his drink for another one, and continued. 'Now. You did agree to put in a hundred and twenty-five pounds. If you could make that two-fifty I'll get down on my knees – now – and lick each of your boots in turn.'

William, sipping what proved to be only a warm tonic water, closed his eyes to indicate that he was taking shrewd stock of the situation, and made a quick review of his financial position. He had eight hundred pounds in his deposit account, most of it left to him by his mother. Two hundred was earmarked for a family holiday in Ireland where he understood *objets d'art* and cottage furniture could still be picked up at bargain prices. He owed a little money to the Inland Revenue. The rest was for emergencies. He had already decided to invest in *Lost*, although he privately doubted that he would have much of a profit to show after writing off Pringle's debts to the Bucket Shop as a condition of contract. An investment of £250 would swell his dividends but then it would also double the risk. He bit his lip judiciously, not sure whether to stick at his original £125 or go the whole hog and offer Pringle £500.

'Incidentally, you were talking about borrowing the flat,' said Pringle. 'I've got you a key. Do you want it tonight?'

'In fact I was thinking of Wednesday evening.'

'Whenever you like – *I'm* never there. Be my guest. Only I don't want to rush you, but all these bods are waiting for me in the Trattoria. I'd ask you to come over and meet them but we've got this high-powered producer character with us. And then of course I've got to dash around the West End raising the loot. So the question is, are you still interested, and if so, could you give me a cheque now?'

'I'm still interested,' said William. 'But I haven't got my . . .'

Pringle whipped out his own cheque book and rested it on the back of a man picking the gristle out of a steak sandwich at the bar. 'Just cross out Lloyds Bank, put the name of your own bank and initial it. If this chap doesn't mind me using him as a writing bureau. Make it out to Lost Productions Ltd – no, better still, make it out to Cash. It's the eighteenth,' he added helpfully as William hesitated.

William wrote the cheque. To his surprise Pringle kissed him full on the lips and then, scattering drinkers on all sides, rushed out of the club.

8

'Hello, is Mr Pringle back yet, please?'
   'Who wants him?'
   'The feet.'
   'Speaking, my flower.'

9

It was five in the morning when William got home. In Tulip Street some men were unloading camera equipment from a green BBC van, and a man in a duffel-coat, who William supposed was the director, was lining up a shot of the street at dawn. William watched for a few minutes, regretting that the tubbed bay tree had been stolen from his doorstep, for he had discerned that the BBC men were shooting a documentary about the migration of the artistic element from Chelsea to Fulham. 'This man is a fashionable antique dealer. He came to Tulip Street because it offered a challenge. Could the public school man and the plumber live side by side? Even more important, what had they to offer each other?' Perhaps when he had slept for a while he would introduce the BBC men to the Bucket Shop and they would take pictures of the Edwardian milk float which he had got in the window but could not get out again. (The potential purchasers, the owners of Trousers Primarily, had wanted to drape it with ties and sweaters in the window of their own establishment; they had settled for a Victorian rocking horse bought from someone else.)

William was rather drunk. After Pringle had dashed out of Kemble's Club he had remained at the bar sipping his tonic water until the proprietor manoeuvred his way towards him and said with great good humour:

'Excuse me, *sir*, but that gentleman over there seems to think you've got his drink.'

A Negro actor, the one who had told the joke about the Pope, was glowering at William.

'I'm terribly sorry. In fact it's only tonic water.'

'Yes, but the point is it's his drink, don't you see? Even if it was a glassful of piss, which it probably tastes like, he paid for it and you're drinking it. You're not a member, are you?'

'No. I was meeting Mr Pringle here.'

'Yes, but he's gone, hasn't he? And Mr Pringle wasn't strictly entitled to bring you in because Mr Pringle hasn't paid his subscription and if I may say so has got a bar bill as long as your arm. So I'm very sorry, I'll have to ask you to leave.'

'It's all right, Robbie, he's with me!'

William saw a long tapered hand with silver varnished nails floundering in the sea of faces. Jackie Douglas, the girl with the large red mouth, elbowed herself towards the bar, smiling vividly at a man who made a coarse remark comparing her breasts with billhooks. 'And we'll both have an extremely large vodka, on my bill.'

'With a gullet like yours, dear, I should think you'd need the whole bottle. You,' said the proprietor with real anthropological interest, 'have a mouth exactly like a pelican.' He withdrew behind the bar. Jackie flashed William a huge set smile.

'He's always like that. He's a poppet, really.'

'It was very kind of you to come to my rescue.'

'Don't thank me, darling, I'm only too delighted to see a friendly face. They're a lovely crowd down here but when they're that way out they can be absolute pigs. You're not in the business, are you?'

'The business of . . .?'

'Obviously not. Show business, as they say. The living theatre.'

'Ah. No.'

'You're just a sleeping partner? Don't think I'm making filthy suggestions.'

William had never quite adjusted himself to the kind of woman who could mention sex flippantly as if it were common ground that neither party to the conversation was a virgin. He answered stiltedly: 'Not at all. In fact the theatre is rather a mystery to me really.'

'We oughtn't to be here, then. Robbie loathes serving people who aren't in the business.'

At Jackie's suggestion they went to another, less specialized club in Charing Cross Road. 'You can't buy a drink, darling, because you're not a member, but if you give me some money I can get them.' This club was similar to Kemble's, but on the first floor, and empty. Jackie again ordered extremely large vodkas, defined here as trebles – somewhat to William's dismay, for he had been expecting food at Pringle's party and had not eaten.

'Cheers, darling. Now tell me all about yourself.'

'What shall I tell you?'

'We know you're not in the theatre, we've got as far as that. What do you do?'

'I'm an antique dealer.'

'How super.'

'It's just a job.' William drew breath to qualify his modesty at length. He did not know yet that Jackie regarded a pause as a verbal hole to be filled immediately with speech. As he opened his mouth she was already speaking.

'My mother nearly married an antique dealer. Justin Lee? In the Burlington Arcade?' The American inflection returned

28

and then vanished again as Jackie launched into a lengthy saga about her mother, her own equivocal relationship with her mother, and her mother's friends. 'She's a poppet, she really is, but sometimes she can be an absolute bitch. You see her marriage was broken up by an actress and so she didn't want me to be one and so then I had this success with the high camp production of *The Student Prince* in the States and she changed her mind, so then I came home and was out of work and she changed her mind again and she has this friend who runs this old-fashioned English cake shop. Mrs Wallace? In Baker Street? You wouldn't know her. She's sweet although she can be a cow, and so I help her out when I'm not working ...'

With no real tale of his own to tell, he was content enough to lie back in this running bath of words. The sensation was in fact a pleasant one, for so long as Jackie continued to talk he was relieved of the great effort of impressing his personality upon her. William, sometimes suspecting that his life lacked substance and direction, did not care to define his character for the enlightenment of others.

'It sounds a dull job and I suppose it would be for anyone doing it regularly but the fascinating thing is all the different people who come into the shop for their little Chelsea buns or whatever ...'

They had more vodka. It had begun to affect William's vision and by now Jackie's face was becoming a white, blurred moon against which the slithering red lips stood out in shiny relief. Jackie was talking now about her career and listing eight productions for which she had nearly been cast since the high camp production of *The Student Prince,* with some account of the circumstances in which she had been finally turned down in each case. William, responding listlessly to every third or fourth sentence, grasped that in the last three years she had done two cat food commercials, another for a beefstock cube that was never shown, and two weeks as holiday relief wardrobe mistress in a small repertory company. She had been working regularly in Mrs Wallace's English cake shop for the past eighteen months on the understanding that she could leave without notice if a professional engagement offered itself. As far as William could gather, this was not an immediate prospect.

The mouth hypnotized him. By now it was the only feature of Jackie's face that was visible to him. Her lips gyrated like an animated neon sign, describing circles, ovals, arcs, ellipses, epicycles. Obscene conjectures began to enter William's mind as he wondered what she was like in bed. It would be, he mused with a flash of drunken imagery that pleased him, like trying to kiss Piccadilly Circus.

It was midnight and the club was closing. They went on to a night club where Jackie was greeted as an old friend by the management. This too was deserted except for a line of sullen hostesses in satin and lamé, and the waiters restlessly patrolling their stations as if still expecting an ambush by bright young things. Despite again not being a member William was allowed to buy a bottle of champagne and some Benson and Hedges cigarettes. He had never been to a night club before and, once the bill had been shown to him by torchlight, resolved never to enter one again. An economic factor supplemented his earlier erotic musings: the proposition that as he was paying for a good time he might as well have it. Diffidently, while Jackie declared a short truce in her verbal onslaught to sip her champagne, he prepared the ground by asking if she lived by herself.

'Always have done, darling, ever since I was eighteen. The thing about sharing flats with other girls is that although it's very nice and very cosy and very chummy you don't really have a place to call your own, and if you *do* want to take anyone back, not that I make a habit of it . . .'

This sounded promising. After an interval during which he learned something of Jackie's friends who had shared flats with each other to their mutual distress, he asked heavily, looking at his watch: 'And where do you live, so all alone?'

Jackie told him about the flat she had in a basement in Marylebone Lane, about the flat she had occupied before that in West Kensington, why she had chosen the flat in Marylebone Lane in preference to another one near Earls Court tube station and a third in the Cromwell Road; how she would have preferred a mews house in Chelsea which a friend could have got for her at a low rent; and how the best flat she had seen recently was a penthouse in Cumberland Place owned by another friend.

By three a.m. the hostesses had gone and the waiters moved pointedly along the lines of tables adjusting chairs and wiping ashtrays that had not been used. William now felt ill, bored and tired, his head throbbed and the prospect of taking Jackie to bed was becoming a matter for exhaustive concentration.

'I think it's high time I was taking you home.'

'Is your family waiting up for you?' asked Jackie, who from the start of the evening had taken it as read that William was married.

'I sincerely hope not.'

'Why don't we get something to eat? I'm famished.'

They went to an all-night steak house in Leicester Square, where Jackie took as her theme her various men friends, many of whom seemed to be gown manufacturers. Some coffee and a mini-steak removed William's nausea, but with it went the last trace of his lascivious fancies. He brought Jackie's discourse to an end by standing up and remaining standing until she gathered up her handbag and led the way out of the restaurant.

He felt sleepy in the taxi to Marylebone Lane, but Jackie's head was leaning on his shoulder and he judged that as an actress she would expect him to kiss her. He had drunk a great deal and he wondered, if circumstance followed circumstance as seemed likely, whether he would be up to his obligations. He approached the substantial lips gingerly, as if edging into a swamp. Immediately the lower part of his face was enveloped in the cavernous mouth; the lips were wet and cold like fresh fish; but he was encouraged to feel his pulse faintly stirring again.

'You're sweet,' said Jackie, and to the taxi driver: 'Here will do.'

William expected that she would invite him in on the pretext of offering him coffee; he was not sure that he could accept for it was very late, the drink swilled inside him and he was still not completely certain of his capabilities. He was very surprised when Jackie scribbled something on an empty cigarette packet, kissed him on the cheek, pushed it into his hand and got out of the cab. 'That's my number, and my number at work. Don't forget to call me, will you?'

10

The purpose of the BBC camera team was to take film of Tulip Street for the credit titles of a play about Borstal. It was not this affront to the prestige of his property that filled William with gloom but the fact that Melisande had botched a film test. As an investor in the theatre he had taken it upon himself, in the early afternoon, to stroll out into the street and chat to some of the BBC men. 'Have you ever worked with Desmond Higgins at all? He did a piece called *Lost* at Barons Court.' Melisande was allowed to join a group of urchins who were being coached in a traditional street game unknown to any of them. After a time the man in the duffel coat called through a megaphone: 'Could we lose the little girl who's crying, please?' One of the BBC men explained tactfully that Melisande was not snotty-nosed enough for their purposes, but William's theory was that she was too stilted and self-conscious and also that when she began to cry she sounded like Stan Laurel.

'... And so now the Chief Mumpkin was very angry indeed. He growled and growled and ... Melisande, are you listening?'

'Yes, Daddy.'

'Why was the Chief Mumpkin angry?'

'I don't know, daddy.'

'I've just explained to you why the Chief Mumpkin was angry. Now you say you were listening to the story – tell me why the Chief Mumpkin was so angry.'

Melisande assumed a wooden expression. William appealed to Poodle. 'You see, there's no point in talking to her. I try to tell her a story and she simply stares out of the window.'

'She's only looking at the camera people. It's interesting for her.'

'It's *interesting* for me, daddy.'

'Yes, and when I took you out there you cried to come in. And now you tell me you want a story but when I rack my brains and think of one you don't listen to it.'

'I *was* listening.'

'Then why was the Chief Mumpkin angry?'

'He was cross.'

'I know he was cross, chum, and daddy's getting cross too. I want to know *why* he was cross.'

'Because of the Tiger.'

'What about the Tiger?'

'He was cross with the Tiger.'

'Why was he cross with the Tiger?'

Melisande was on the brink of tears. William recognized the signs – a fixed smile contradicted by a reddening of the cheeks and a quivering of the chin – and tried to fight back a wave of irritation.

'Because Tigger went up the tree when – when – when Christopher Robin told him not to.'

'Oh, for *goodness* sake?' William threw up his hands. 'Is she like this at school? Can she take *anything* in at all? I'm telling her a perfectly straightforward Mumpkin story, she swears she's listening to it . . .'

'Leave her *alone*, William!'

'. . . and she comes out with some twaddle about Christopher Robin. I'm quite ready to leave her alone but if she wants a story why doesn't she listen to it? Why does she imagine she's listening to Winnie the Pooh?'

'Because to begin with all the stories you tell her are *from* Winnie the Pooh.'

'Nonsense.'

'They *are*, William. You just alter Poor Bear or whatever he's called to, I don't know, Chief Munchkin, and you think you're inventing a . . . No wonder she's mixed up.'

'That's why I'm mixed up, Daddy. Because you turn Pooh Bear into the Chief Mumpkin.'

'Yes, well I think mummy can tell you a story in future.'

As soon as Melisande had gone to bed Poodle asked abruptly:

'Did you give her any pocket money this week?'

'No, she didn't ask for any. Why?'

Poodle's question induced in William the distinct tightening of the stomach muscles that he always experienced when his daughter was under discussion. The pocket money question, particularly, was one he did not want to think about. He had once read in a digest an article by a popular psychologist on the dangers of doling out pocket money that had not been earned; the gift of money, the psychologist implied, was a substitute for the gift of love, and the shrewd child would soon realize that she was being compensated in half crowns for what she was denied in parental affection. Although William had no high opinion of his daughter's shrewdness he drew up a tariff of household chores ranging from bed-making (sixpence) to shelling peas (a shilling, but apparently an obsolescent task). There were several quarrels with Melisande about her failure to honour their contract, then William read in another magazine that some modern parents were exploiting their children to an extent unheard of since *The Water Babies* and that pocket money was a right and not a privilege. This caused a dilemma in his mind which he resolved by ignoring the pocket money motif altogether and giving Melisande half a crown only when she asked for it, which was not often.

Poodle said:

'You didn't give her a ten shilling note?'

'Of course I didn't. Why?'

'I found a ten shilling note in her purse. She said at first you'd given it to her but when I said I'd ask you about it she said she'd found it in the street.'

'Probably she did. It probably belongs to one of those BBC people.'

'That's what I thought but why should she say you gave it to her?'

'Why does she say anything? Why does she say she's listening to a story when she isn't? Why does she run the taps and wet the soap instead of washing her hands?'

'Don't you think you'd better find out whom it belongs to?'

'You don't imagine I'm going to walk up and down the street asking that crowd if any of them's lost ten shillings, do you? I should think none of them knows to the nearest fiver what he's got in his pockets.'

'Anyway, I've told her I'm going to give it to Oxfam.'

Not caring to think about Melisande any more, he fell to day-dreaming about his outing with Jackie. He had been looking forward to this all afternoon and had prepared a rough mental list of the highlights of his adventure (being picked up by a West End actress, drinking champagne with her in a Mayfair night club, kissing her in a taxi on the way to her London flat) so that he could dwell on them at leisure. But he found it difficult to recapture the mood of speculative excitement in which he had returned to Tulip Street in the early hours. Wanting to remember a stimulating evening in promising company he could recall only a vast cornucopian mouth spilling out an endless pot-pourri of nouns, adjectives and verbs. He began to think about Rosemary.

Soon Poodle said:

'By the way, what time did you get home last night?'

'About two, why?'

'It must have been a good party.'

'Routine.'

'And who do you say gave it?'

'A man called Pringle. He comes into the shop sometimes. I think you might have met him.'

'I might have done. I don't know.'

11

Rosemary, as William had been the first to reassure her, was not a nymphomaniac. This was one evening between the Epping Forest and Hyde Park fiascos and their perilous interlude at the Bucket Shop. Rosemary wanted to make love in an abandoned prefab off the Cromwell Road extension; William demurred; Rosemary insisted; William outlined the risks to which they would expose themselves; Rosemary begged him to forget caution and consider urgent physical need; William refused; Rosemary became introspective and wondered aloud if she ought to see a doctor or a psychiatrist. William consoled her by pointing out (he had been reading the serialization of an American book about man's primeval impulses) that it was her thirst for adventure rather than for sex that was insatiable.

This was true. Rosemary's early life was a catalogue of midnight feasts, raided orchards and roof-top escapades. That word 'escapade', along with 'madcap', 'tomboy', 'exploit', 'scrape', featured regularly in her reading at that time. She married principally because her parents were opposed to the match, and on the promise of a runaway honeymoon; she became unfaithful to her husband in order to keep her wits sharp and her days full. Rosemary had once heard a semi-drunken peer say on television that marriage without infidelity was like a salad without dressing. This so completely matched her own view that she set off at once to interview him for her magazine in the hope that their spiritual affinity might become temporal. The peer quickly admitted to being a homosexual but Rosemary was not unduly disappointed, for as the headmaster of a boy's grammar school had said on the same programme, it was better to travel hopefully than to arrive. In William Rosemary possessed the nearest human equivalent to the Inner Circle.

'This Pringle. Isn't he the photographer who was in the Bucket Shop, the day we first met?'

'Yes. Why, are you nervous in case we run into him?'

'No, it's just that I see him sometimes in pubs in Fleet Street when I go for a drink with Robin. I wouldn't want him coming up and saying, "How do you like my flat?"'

'He doesn't know it's you I'm taking there – he imagines you're just some anonymous girl I've picked up somewhere.'

'How horrible.'

'I know, but I didn't want to involve you. As far as risk is concerned I'm the only one that's running any, because he knows Poodle, or at least I believe he's met her. But would you rather call the whole thing off?'

"Don't be silly. I've been looking forward to it all week.'

They approached the house where Pringle lived by a devious route, for it was off a main road in Chelsea quite close to Melisande's school and Poodle knew several mothers in the district. Having reached the premises unobserved William hustled Rosemary up the path as if he were a policeman escorting his charge through a gauntlet of press photographers at the entrance to an assize court. The key fitted, the door did not behave eccentrically and refuse to open, and there were no stray and curious tenants loitering on the threshold; several of William's main fears were thus initially disposed of.

In the bare hall, however, his nervousness returned. A woman, possibly Pringle's landlady, was putting out milk bottles at the top of the stairs leading down to the basement. She looked at William and Rosemary speculatively but said nothing. William hovered, thinking that perhaps he ought to explain his presence. 'What floor is Mr Pringle on?' he was about to ask, but then Rosemary pulled at his sleeve and led him boldly upstairs. 'The thing on these occasions,' she said, taking Pringle's key from him, 'is to look as if you own the place.'

Pringle's flat was no more than one of a number of single rooms on the third floor, with a shared bathroom. William's first alarmed reaction was that Rosemary was very likely to go wandering out on to the landing stark naked, looking for the lavatory. He glanced around the room and noted a number of objects rightfully belonging to the Bucket Shop and which he had written off as having been broken in transit. On the bed was a scrawled postcard:

Sorry for a bad start but something has cropped up. Can you possibly be out by eight at latest? I have *got* to come back with someone – business – and don't want any evidence there was anyone here. Make sure she doesn't leave her knickers under the pillow, lock door and tear this up. P.

'Oh God.'

'It still gives us an hour,' said Rosemary. She had read the card over William's shoulder (to his embarrassment, owing to the reference to knickers) and was already undressing.

'But it's quarter past seven already,' said William, looking at his watch. It was five past, but Rosemary was already discarding her own watch and also her engagement ring, although not her wedding ring. She placed them methodically on a shelf near the sink, as Poodle always did in Tulip Street when she was about to do the washing up or stuff a chicken. The chicken-stuffing parallel was the one that lodged in William's mind, and he found it dispiriting. 'What if he comes back early?'

'Why should he do that?' said Rosemary carelessly. 'He says be out by eight – he'll give us a quarter of an hour margin at least.'

'I would think he means to come *back* at eight. "Be out by eight at latest." He means that we should give *him* a quarter of an hour margin.'

'Whoever gives *who* a quarter of an hour, the worst thing that can happen is he'll come back while we're still here. You're paying half his rent – what does he expect?'

Rosemary had taken off her dress and shoes and stockings, and was now, with an undignified wriggle, peeling off her girdle. William was dismayed by her audacity but at the same time disappointed in the humdrum manner of her disrobing. Rosemary often stimulated her hours with William by describing to him in detail what they would do when they were alone. They sometimes passed along the Kings Road together when William would linger by the windows of expensive antique shops in the belief that he was studying the market; Rosemary would enliven these interludes by expressing a wish to be made love to on a Regency dining table or in a quilted leather porter's chair. The discrepancy between her eroticism then and her cool objectivity now did nothing for William's desire which was already diminished by his anxiety about Pringle's return. He fiddled dismally with the postcard while Rosemary tried to unknot his tie.

'You see, Rosemary, he has someone with him. "I have *got*," underlined, "to come back with someone."'

'He's bringing a girl back, that's all. Stand still.'

'He says business.'

'He means a girl. If it comes to it she'll be as embarrassed as you will. As *we* will. And anyway *if* it comes to it the door's locked and they won't be able to get in.'

'He has another key.'

'There's a bolt.'

'I'm still not very happy about it.'

His tie was fastened in an old-fashioned Windsor knot and Rosemary had only succeeded in pulling it tighter. William sat miserably on the bed and, re-adjusting his collar, glanced surreptitiously at his watch. There was still a clear fifty minutes before Pringle's return and it was of course unlikely that he might come back unexpectedly early, but William could not explain to Rosemary that this remote probability was only the touchpaper to the powder keg, or rather the magazine, of his anxieties. If he did not have to return home to Poodle or if he could return home without the necessity for social intercourse with her; if Rosemary were not married or if she had a broad-minded husband; if there were no possibility of her becoming pregnant; if she were not likely to scratch his back or leave teeth-marks on his shoulder; if, made reckless by his ardour, she might not threaten to leave her husband or beg him to leave his wife; if the landlady might not burst in or one of Pringle's neighbours might not knock on the door to borrow sugar or one of his creditors to recover a debt; if William and Rosemary were in Bristol or preferably Bali, neither of them married and with the reservations conditional both to the Bristol venture and the escapade now in progress all observed, then William might have been aroused by the deeply-breathing, now naked figure on the bed.

He kissed her wholeheartedly in order to prevent her unbuttoning his shirt.

'Don't you honestly think we ought to go?'

'You'd say that if we were locked in a safe in the Bank of England. Put your hand there.'

Listening keenly, he was able to hear footsteps outside and a key scraping in a lock. Clearly the sound came from the room across the landing but it was enough for William.

'If you're not leaving, Rosemary, I am. It's all right you being so bloody blasé about it – you were just the same when we went to the Bucket Shop that night, and you knew Poodle might turn up but you didn't care. When I make love to you I simply don't want to be worrying about somebody who might come crashing in. And if that makes me hyper-bloody-sensitive, I'm sorry.'

Rosemary dressed in silence and with irritating care. They walked to Earls Court, the invisible frontier post defining the borders of William's Fulham and Rosemary's Kensington. William expected a reprisal: a hint that she was on the verge of an affair with someone else or that her husband was on heat. She was unusually silent. He thought, and half-hoped, that she despaired of his temerity and that this was the finish. But before leaving Rosemary said:

'So it's all on to Bristol, then?'

'I've been thinking about that. I honestly don't see how I can get there.'

'You did promise.'

'I know, but it's very difficult. I don't see how I can leave the shop on Saturday, my busiest day.'

'But we'll go to Pringle's again, won't we? I mean he won't be coming back early *every* night.'

'My view is that he will. I think he's that kind of person. I'm a bit off Pringle's flat, to tell you the truth.'

'You're a funny fellow, William.'

12

'Kiss them,' said Poodle.

'Kiss what?'

'My feet. You said I had beautiful feet.'

13

'*Size u massenea da cowl poy inna freej, koshe fingsea sorf.*'

William was cheered to find Poodle out but incensed by the presence of Lil, the thirteen-year-old baby-sitter from next door. Everything about Lil irritated him, from her archetypal cockney name to her anomalous (at a time when Tulip Street was flocking to the cheap boutiques) cast-off, shin-length clothes. She not only retained a Liza of Lambeth accent in face of the class-levelling influence of television, but seemed to be engaged in active field-work towards preserving the speech of Bow Bells. The subtleties of Tulip Street's changing social climate eluded her and she insisted on regarding William's family (her own father was a chimney sweep) as no different from her own, except in that it was smaller by five units.

Lil and Melisande were playing ludo on the floor. William gave them a disapproving glance. He could not see why his daughter, at her age, should not be playing chess.

'*Jeer?*'

'Do I hear what?' he said distastefully.

'*Size us massenea da cowl poy inna freej, koshe fingsea sorf.*'

He translated.

'I mustn't eat the cold pie in the fridge why?'

'*Koshe fingsea sorf.*'

'Because she thinks it's off. Thank you.'

Melisande, gawping up from the ludo board with a fair imitation of Lil's squint, said: 'Where you bin, ded?'

'You don't mean, "Where've you been, daddy?" by any remote chance?'

'Yes, daddy.'

'Then isn't that perhaps what you'd better say?'

'Where've you bin, daddy?'

'*Been.*'

'Been.'

'That's better. Have you eaten?'

'*Yair,*' put in Lil. '*She zadder negg, encha, Melly?*'

Shuddering at the contraction, William repaired to another room, where he tried to interest himself in a library book throwing a new light on the assassination of Mahatma Ghandi. But he could not read for thinking about his evening with Rosemary and worrying that she probably thought he had become impotent.

Presently Poodle came home, carefully flaunting a circular advertising a meeting of the parent-teacher association. William pretended to be deep in his book to avoid conversation, for anything to do with Melisande's education gave him an actual pain in the stomach.

Poodle went to bed. William put his book aside and began to reconstruct the events of the evening with the purpose of editing them towards his own advantage. He re-traced the detour round Melisande's school to the street where Pringle lived, recoiling now in horror at the thought that Poodle had been in that district all the time. When he reached the point where he and Rosemary had hurried up the path and entered the house, he recalled that Rosemary had gone ahead of him up the stairs and without any direction from him had made straight for Pringle's room, which she must have visited before.

14

Upstairs, Poodle undressed with the self-conscious narcissism of one who has just come sexually of age. She was pleased, not disappointed, that Pringle had not shown himself to be the versatile lover she had conjectured him to be. He was experienced enough to satisfy her immediate needs but not imaginative enough to make her feel gauche in their fulfilment. The exploration of her new maturity would be a profitable adventure for both of them. She did not want Pringle's company, his conversation or his love – only his practical help and technical advice. It would be the relationship of an experimenter of vision and a proficient laboratory assistant. Poodle believed herself to be at last unique.

15

'So in effect you *had* been there before.'

'As far as the threshold. As soon as he opened the door of his room I knew what he was up to and I wouldn't go in.'

'Then why did you say that you'd never been there before?'

'I never said that. I just didn't bother to say that I had.'

'But you said you didn't know him.'

'I *didn't* know him, William. When I met him in the Bucket Shop that day I'd never . . .'

'No, but after that. You said you sometimes saw him in Fleet Street . . .'

'. . . and that I was afraid of him coming up to Robin and me and talking about us, *you* and me, borrowing his room. But I don't *know* him. I just know him to speak to.'

'All right. So you say you came across him at this press conference . . .'

'I don't *say* I did. I *did*.'

'. . . and he offered you a lift home. What in?'

'His car, of course.'

'He doesn't have a car.'

'A taxi, then. I've forgotten. Doesn't *that* show you I don't know him all that well?'

'. . . . and having accepted a lift home in what you now say was a taxi, you went instead to his room?'

'Not to his room. To his door. He said he had this book I might like to borrow and it was only when I got to the threshold . . .'

'I'm sorry, Rosemary, but I just don't believe you.'

'You'll have to unbelieve me, then, won't you?'

16

The quarrel with Rosemary happened shortly before his thirty-sixth birthday. He was apprehensive that she might extend the olive branch in the shape of an unsolicited greetings telegram or a present delivered to his home. He still remembered Christmas Eve, when he had had to cancel a celebration drink with Rosemary for some reason or other: she took a cab to Tulip Street and posted a pair of cufflinks anonymously through the letter box. They were found by Melisande who made an embarrassing song-and-dance about Santa Claus fetching Christmas presents for the grown-ups.

But his birthday brought nothing from Rosemary. Poodle gave him a picture of a steam engine woven in silk which she had picked up in the Portobello Road. She told William that if he did not like it she would not be offended if he sold it in the shop. It was so beautiful that he did so immediately, pricing it at three pounds and selling it for two. Poodle did not tell him that this was just over a third what she had paid for it.

Melisande presented him with a birthday card which she had made herself. He had a poor opinion of the craftsmanship employed, and there were three spelling mistakes. He felt once again a sense of injustice that providence had not asked him to guide the future of a more promising child.

William's birthday fell at the end of the fiscal year and so it was usual for him on this occasion to take stock of his metaphysical as well as his financial balance sheets. He was, as always, dismayed. He seemed to have travelled far, but on some devious route that had doubled back almost to the point at which he began. He felt the ennui that follows a long period of activity but he could not bring to mind anything concrete that he had achieved. He had the impression of having frittered away his time and dissipated his energies in the pursuit of fripperies. His conclusion was that at thirty-six he had had too much of too little.

He had always seen himself as a man of moderate dreams and modest appetites. It had once seemed a reasonable ambition to have his own small business, to own a compact, comfortable house in a fashionable area, and to command the love of a vivacious wife and of a dutiful daughter. But the simple path that he had mapped out for himself had turned into a maze of dead-ends and roundabouts. The Bucket Shop did not thrive, his wife was shrewish, his daughter was irritating, and the house in Tulip Street had become a millstone around his neck. He put part of the blame upon himself, recognizing that perhaps he lacked the stature of a man of business and the solidarity of a man of property. Sometimes he tried to see these deficiencies as advantages, when he would pose to himself as a contented man, widely misunderstood, who had opted out of the rat-race.

But the kaleidoscopic nature of his own personality worried him too. He was apt to wake up in the morning resolving to change his character as another man might decide to change his suit: in future he would become more tolerant towards his daughter, more attentive to his wife; he would abandon Rosemary and become more discerning in his business. The only effect of these decisions was to make him feel more than ever that his world, like the surface of the sun, was made up of rapidly transmuting gases. Alarmed and bewildered, William would retreat to the path he had made for himself, finding what sense of direction he might in its familiar cul-de-sacs and detours.

In cheerful moments he put himself down as a mental hypochondriac; in times of depression he was convinced that fate worked against him. Yet he found it difficult to trace any real pattern of ill-luck in his life. Indeed his plans often seemed to be attended in their execution by great good fortune: the perplexing thing was that in their accomplishment they were always somehow off-true to the original blueprint. The Bucket Shop, for example: he had been fortunate in finding a shop at a low rent; his mother's death had given him capital when he needed it; he had often been incredibly lucky in buying in ignorance some ephemeral stock that suddenly became the vogue. Yet for all the care he lavished on the shop it lacked the magpie attractiveness of its rivals. He spent many hours dressing and re-dressing the window, hampered it was true by the Edwardian milk float that had been lodged there for the last six months; he gave a considerable part of each day to arranging his stock on butcher's blocks and along the crowded walls. Then Pringle came along and told him that the final effect was of the spare room of a Victorian seaside brothel. William had to concede that something had gone wrong somewhere. It was in every respect the shop he had imagined in his mind's eye – but out of focus, as if the retina were faulty.

The house, too, had been an opportune purchase. He had been able to snap it up, after all, for half the price of its Chelsea counterparts and there was still a possibility that one day the window cleaners and chimney sweeps might move out or die and Tulip Street would become a prosperous neighbourhood. The rooms were warm and well-proportioned, with nooks and crannies of great character. They were decorated to William's taste: old maps on the walls, converted oil-lamps and button-back chairs, and a scrubbed refectory table in the kitchen. But here too there was an indefinable discrepancy between conception and achievement. William put it down at first to his family's untidiness: Poodle's annoying practice of leaving the cellophane wrappings from cigarette packets on tables or shelves, and Melisande's habit of dropping pieces of broken plastic about the floor. He had sharp words with them both and they began to use the waste paper basket. Then William decided that the house lacked atmosphere: he raided the Bucket Shop and brought home art nouveau sweetmeat dishes to use as ash-trays, sporting mugs for the bookshelves, a stuffed fish for the bathroom and a pedlar doll for the sitting-room mantelpiece. It was in vain. His antique shop might look like a junkyard but his home now looked like an antique shop. Melisande began to play with the miniature wares belonging to the pedlar doll and lost some of them; the stuffed fish fell down; cellophane wrappings and sweet papers littered the coffee tables again, and William, despairing, left the creative running of the house to Poodle.

'I'm sorry you didn't like the silk picture I bought you. It would have looked nice in the hall.'

'I liked it very much, but you said I ought to sell it.'

'No, I said you could sell it if ... It doesn't matter. You don't feel like apologizing to Melisande, do you?'

'For what?'

'You were perfectly horrible to her about her birthday card. She spent a whole afternoon making it and all you could do was to stand over her making her spell "happy" over and over again until she burst into tears.'

'She's nine years old, Poodle. Do you want her to grow up totally illiterate? And incidentally, if you want something to hang up in the hall, what's wrong with those old steel engravings? I fetched them home three weeks ago and I don't recollect that you've looked at them yet.'

'If you mean those pictures of the Crystal Palace and so

on you cut out of the *Illustrated London News,* I'd frankly far rather see *The Stag At Bay* or *Bubbles* on the wall.'

'Which says a great deal for your taste, because both happen to be very fashionable pictures at the moment.'

He did not like Poodle to interrupt his thoughts: she rubbed him up the wrong way and made him feel embittered. She could so easily have become what he wanted her to be – not necessarily an artist or a sculptress but a person of flair. She could have mixed martinis for him when he came home, surprised him with clever touches of interior decorating, and given small dinner parties. William rarely invited anyone home nowadays, partly because he seemed to have lost touch with all the people that once he might have called his friends, partly because introducing his wife by her nickname had become an embarrassment. It was not that she had grown out of it: she had never lived up to it. He suspected that people were disappointed when they met her.

For the same reason he regretted having christened his daughter Melisande. The name suggested an elfin precociousness, a round-eyed sophistication that was simply not present in the lumpish creature that Melisande had become. William often felt wretched about the way he treated her, but he knew that he could not help himself. He still hoped that by shouting at her he might cause her IQ to rise like mercury in a thermometer on a hot day. Again he put much of the blame on himself, but a lot of it on Poodle: they were not a family and they did not lead a family life. Sometimes he read the autobiographies of famous men in the Sunday newspapers: he would grow wistful over the descriptions of intelligent dinner table conversation, of the intellectual mothers and political grandmothers who read *Tristam Shandy* aloud to their offspring, and the news that poured into these families of sons and brothers who had won the Newdigate Prize. It was too late for that now, and in any case Melisande lacked the application for scholarship. But there were other autobiographies, of men and women who had been block-headed while young but who remembered a corporate golden childhood of rides in the landau to grandmama's, seaside villas

rented for the summer, and fallen apples on the lawn. Here
too Melisande had let him down. She suffered from hay fever,
and also she would not eat cake or strawberries. In consequence there had been no picnics on the river and no idyllic
teas at Fortnum and Mason's.

William had always felt completely justified in turning to
a mistress, for he felt that he had given respectability its
chance. Before Rosemary there had been nobody but Poodle;
before Poodle there had only been a scuffled intrigue with a
W.R.A.F officer in his air force days and a barely-consummated
passion for a nurse when he first came to live in London. He
entered into his affair with Rosemary shortly after his thirty-
fifth birthday: he could remember having taken stock of his
life then and the feeling of disillusion, guilt and frustration,
totalling to a restless melancholy, that had led him to her. He
was somewhat disconcerted now to realize that instead of les-
sening, his depression had merely spread thinner, to encom-
pass Rosemary and his disappointment in her.

17

'Miss Jackie Douglas? This is William.'

'William who?'

'You remember. We met at Kemble's Club.'

'I'm still no nearer, darling. Ask me another.'

'You thought I had money in *Apart From That, Mrs Lincoln* and it turned out . . .'

'Oh, *that* William. When are you taking me out to dinner?'

18

'Are you having an affair with somebody?' asked Poodle as
he brushed dandruff from his shoulders.

He met his own glance in the mirror and worked on his
face-muscles until he had restored an expression neutral to

the point of blankness. He was unable to make the same adjustment to his voice and it quavered slightly as he said:

'What a curious thing to ask.'

'Would you tell me if you were?'

'I don't know why you're bringing this up. It's a hypothetical question, surely.'

'For the past year you seem to have been coming home later and later two and sometimes three times a week. What keeps you till eight and nine o'clock in the evening?'

'I do work for a living,' said William, the voice now under control. 'If I'm not at the shop I could be in a dozen places. Buying, looking at things. If you took any interest in the business you'd know.'

'And then lately you've started disappearing for whole evenings at a time.'

'*One* whole evening at a time, if you mean the party the other night.'

'All right, the party and now this dinner you're supposed to be going to . . .'

By a happy fluke, so William had discovered in *What's On*, the annual dinner of the Society of Young Antique Dealers was being held this evening at the Hilton Hotel. He had joined the Society several months ago on the off-chance that it might provide him with an alibi – a weekend summer school in Bristol perhaps – for an outing with Rosemary.

'If you'd like to ring the Hilton and ask for the banqueting manager . . .'

'I'm sure you'll be there but I'd like to know how long for and where you'll go when you leave. I do happen to know that the party you were supposed to be at didn't go on till two in the morning or anything like it.'

Here the argument ended, William not thinking it prudent to challenge Poodle's sources nor she to reveal them. She suspected about William's evening at Kemble's Club only that he had fallen in with some crowd and got himself drunk, she quite believed that he was off now to the Young Antique Dealers' dinner; but she knew that William was inclined towards the greatest uneasiness even when comparatively innocent, and she was determined that any burden of guilt there may have been built up in Tulip Street should be on his shoulders and not on hers.

As soon as William had gone out Poodle arranged for Lil the babysitter to come in, and then she went round to Pringle's flat.

'I think they're all out upstairs. Who did you want to see?'
'Mr Pringle.'
'Are you the lady that keeps ringing up?'
'I don't suppose I'm the only one.'
'Because I've got to go rushing up to the third landing every time that phone rings. You'll very rarely get him at this time in the evening.'
'I'm sorry. I'll leave him a message.'

If you weren't so busy I'd begin to think you were avoiding me. Your landlady doesn't approve of me ringing you – could you ring me? Daytime between ten and noon is safest. My feet miss you – they've never been loved before.

19

Having intended only to ask Jackie out for a drink William was discomposed when she invited herself to dinner, but not so discomposed as when, just as he was setting off for it, Poodle asked him if he was having an affair. He was trembling as he walked out into Tulip Street. His nervousness caused him to walk with short, rapid steps and he travelled half a mile along the Fulham Road in the wrong direction before pausing by a telephone box to debate with himself how best to get out of his liaison with Jackie.

The institution of suspicion had a shrivelling effect on William. It caused the muscles of his stomach to contract and prompted him to make impetuous decisions to put the past behind him, a course that was not always quickly possible. There had been many painfully frustrating interviews with Rosemary when he had tried to end their relationship after some imagined word of distrust from his wife. He determined that in Jackie's case his best plan would be simply not to turn up at the restaurant where they had agreed to meet; he could then go to the Hilton Hotel and in effect gatecrash the Young Antique Dealers' dinner, remembering to take the menu home with him and leave it in some casual place.

But a sense of decency made him telephone Jackie after all.

'Darling, I'm so glad you called. Are you at Victor's?' – the restaurant where he had booked a table.

'In fact no, I'm still in the Fulham Road. Jackie –'

'.... Because I wonder if you'd mind terribly picking up some Benson and Hedges for me before you go in? I'd get them myself but I'm flat stony broke, and I know Victor doesn't sell them although he used to, and I know it's silly but I do get this terrible throat if I smoke anything else.'

'Yes, Jackie.'

'That's very sweet of you, love.'

'Except that I'm wondering if you'd be very disappointed if we didn't go to Victor's tonight?'

'Of course not! We'll go wherever you like. I only suggested Victor's because they know me there.' And before William could explain that she had misunderstood him, Jackie began to examine alternative venues. She recommended a bistro run by friends of her mother's in Covent Garden, reviewed the limited menu of Kemble's Club where she was sure William would not want to go again, mentioned several establishments to which she had been taken on various occasions and summarized their drawbacks, and finally arranged that they should meet at the original restaurant after all, and if William did not take to it they could always have a drink and then move on.

He was finding that Jackie's conversation had a sapping effect on his willpower. Committed to eat with her after all he made up his mind to get through the meal as quickly as possible and take himself home. But by the time he called for the bill she was in the middle of a long anecdote about an aunt who was being swindled out of some property by a

Hungarian, and by the time she had finished that story and had sketched in the preliminary outlines of its sequel they had drifted – William was not sure how they had got there – into one of her drinking clubs. He now reached the Cinderella conviction that so long as he was home by midnight everything would be all right: there might not be a Hilton menu to show but he would be sober and (provided he put Jackie into a cab to find her own way home) of an innocent demeanour. He might even make love to Poodle to remove her suspicions completely.

It was not quite ten thirty. Jackie's monologue soothed and settled him and he was content to float like driftwood along the various tributaries of her stream of consciousness. He was dimly aware that the aunt and the Hungarian were now minor characters in a longer story about her mother and some fish. Other people and places floated in and out of the narrative: the gown manufacturers who were her friends, Mrs Wallace's cake shop, the flat where she used to live in West Kensington, her fellow actors in the high camp production of *The Student Prince*. To William they had the happy familiarity of a recurrent dream; and as in a dream, one locale melted imperceptibly into another, and he discovered that they were now sitting in a night club. He was anxious but not alarmed, for it was only half past twelve. A glass of champagne and then he would plead a headache and go home.

'Don't whatever you do ask the waiter for aspirins, love – they'll charge you about ten bob in this place. I've got something at home if it's still bad.'

By two a.m., after an Alka-Seltzer he did not want, William was in bed with Jackie.

20

He could not remember ever having been so happy, a discovery that filled him with trepidation. It was not the love-making, although there had been all the moans and cries and gesticulation of the limbs that he had always believed should be his portion. (Jackie's over-generous mouth had featured a good deal in this, and he was rather perturbed about some flesh wounds consistent with having been attacked by a small shark.) But as soon as the lovemaking was over and he began to wonder how to extricate himself without emotional turmoil, Jackie was the one to suggest that it was time for him to leave. She wiped large deposits of lipstick off his face, tied his shoelaces and called a mini-cab. 'Will you be all right, darling? Will your family be worried? Have you got a good excuse?' She fussed over him like a mother seeing off her son at the end of embarkation leave.

William was touched. He blurted out:

'Before I came out tonight my wife asked me if I was having an affair with somebody.'

'Well, you're not, love. I've been around too much to get myself entangled with married men. You know? You're very lovely to me and modest and gentle, unlike some of the bastards I could name, but I don't want to take over anybody else's part in your life.'

'Do I construe that as meaning you'd rather not see me again?'

'I want to see you very much. Call me whenever you like, and believe me I'll drop everything. But I don't want you to think that you have to, and I don't want to be a nuisance to you.'

He arranged that he would telephone her and take her out to dinner the following week. He felt enormously grateful to her. Lulled by the long evening of her talk he had forgotten his earlier misgivings; now, before it had even taken shape, she had anaesthetized the succeeding anxiety he would have felt about being involved with her. William was stirred by intimations of liberty – the kind of liberty he was after when, feeling that he was getting over-engaged with Rosemary, he sought temporary relief from their relationship. Grand, unfocused visions of the possibilities of the future began to form themselves – the delights of parenthood, the quiet domestic evening, the thrust of business endeavour, the pleasures of philandery, all unshadowed by the nagging presence of an over-demanding mistress. He would see Jackie perhaps once a fortnight, occasionally send her flowers and otherwise devote himself to constructive pursuits.

He went home light-hearted, elevated rather than made apprehensive by the rising dawn. It was only as he reached Tulip Street that, out of habit, he began to ask himself introvert questions, and one of them was: Is this all I want? Despite his carefree mood he was despondent beyond measure to realize that it was, insofar as he knew.

21

There was only one piece of unfinished business and that was Rosemary's duplicity with Pringle, for which he was still awaiting a full explanation. While William's affair with Rosemary was irrevocably finished it did not have an ending. His sense of order was disturbed and so, faintly, was his under-developed sense of drama. He felt a need to bring this chapter of his life to a proper climax: explanation, remorse, apology; reproach, forgiveness, magnanimity; and then, when Rosemary meekly bent her forehead for the kiss of absolution, he would smile sadly and walk away. This last action would have to be metaphorical for, bearing in mind her powers of persuasion, he preferred the final scene of their drama to be acted out on the telephone.

Rosemary rang the Bucket Shop several times during the next two days. William offered lame excuses for not being able to see her while at the same time, by the judicious use of pauses, giving her ample opportunity to explain why she had gone with Pringle to his flat and what they had done together while in it. But it was not Rosemary's policy to apologize for past errors and on the fifth time of telephoning William grew angry and told her that he had no wish to see her again.

'Because I don't want to, that's why. I don't trust you, I'm not sure I even like you, and in any case you're married, I'm married and it must be quite plain that the whole thing's surely pointless.'

'That's what I want to talk to you about, William. My husband's found out about us.'

He agreed to meet Rosemary for a drink at the end of his day's work.

22

Poodle had got into the habit of hanging around outside the house where Pringle lived. She arrived each morning at ten past nine after taking Melisande to school and obligingly situated herself across the road where Pringle could see her from his window. The situation was not new to him and his routine was to go down to the basement and into the back garden, scale the wall of the house backing on to it, enter that house by the basement door and, nodding pleasantly to the several Africans who thought he was their landlord, walk out into the next street.

This morning, however, Pringle's landlady was out and so the basement door was locked. He had a ten o'clock appointment in the West End and it was now nine-fifty. A confrontation with Poodle was unthinkable: she plainly wanted to discuss his future intentions and Pringle was not a man with any taste for abstract conversation. He decided to give her fifteen minutes and then, if necessary, admit to himself that a state of siege existed and cancel his appointment. He had some work to do – there were several old photographs needing new captions before he could canvas them again in Fleet Street. He applied himself to this task until nine fifty-five when, since Poodle was still pacing the street, he made a telephone call and altered his appointment to eleven o'clock.

Pringle was a malleable personality and he was always ready to adapt himself to new circumstances. The circumstance now was that he unexpectedly had nearly an hour to spare. He had nothing else to do and he did not care to have time hanging on his hands. He undressed, put on a dressing gown, and then opened the window and whistled to Poodle as one might whistle for a cab. She looked up and pointed to herself, in query; Pringle nodded; and eagerly she ran across the street and entered the house. He was waiting for her at the door of his room. He indicated the bed, she lay down on it and he made love to her. The transaction so exactly fulfilled Poodle's requirements that in due course she exclaimed: 'That was marvellous! It really was!'

'All right, but piss off now, darling, would you? I'm busy,' said Pringle, speaking for the first time.

23

'Never mind what I'm angry about. What's all this about Robin finding out about us?'

'He has, that's all.'

'How?'

'I don't know.'

'For God's sake, Rosemary. Has somebody seen us? Did somebody tell him? Or what?'

Rosemary's eyes became deep pools of misery as the sparkle of excitement in them dissolved, a transition as abrupt as if she had held a loo-mask before her face.

'*I* told him.'

William could not blanch, in that he was ash-white already. In the interim since Rosemary's telephone call he had indulged in exhaustive speculation. The arrival of Robin in Tulip Street to knock him down, the writ for enticement, the heavy damages and eventual bankruptcy, Rosemary's divorce, and presently his own, were no longer spectral possibilities: the dark pattern of the future was already deeply etched. Bleakly he raised his eyes, as simultaneously she lowered hers.

'*Why?*'

'I suppose I was mooching about the house looking miserable because we'd quarrelled and I missed you. He kept on and on asking me what was wrong and so at last I told him about you.'

'By name, I suppose?'

'Not actually.'

He studied Rosemary's face: the sullen jowls, the pouting lips, the lowered eye-lids – in any identity parade of the tragic muses she would have been picked out as the victim, rather than the perpetrator, of disaster. He knew this expression very well. He had seen it when she had something genuinely disturbing to convey, as on the day she had once distressed him by confessing that she had voluntarily lost her virginity at the age of twelve; but it was also a feature of less substantive tidings, when Rosemary made much out of little in order to administer a shock to William's system. He could remember – he had just had to postpone their weekend in Bristol for the third time – Rosemary solemnly announcing that her husband was forcing her to emigrate to Canada; the substance of this was that she had found him reading an article about Vancouver in a newspaper advertising supplement.

William gauged a fractional lightening of his heart equivalent to a cautious suggestion of relief. He spoke carefully.

'When you say "not actually", do you mean that you haven't actually told him about me, or that he doesn't actually know who I am, or what do you mean?'

'I told him there was somebody else.'

'Without mentioning me?'

'No.'

'Let's be quite clear. Are you saying no, you didn't mention me, or no, that's not what you meant?'

'I didn't mention you.'

'And he didn't ask?'

'No.'

'But surely, Rosemary. If my wife told me she was in love with someone else the first thing I'd ask would be . . .'

'It wasn't like that. It was all a sort of joking thing.'

'How the *hell* could it be a sort of joking thing?'

'It was. Robin's like that. He said why was I always miserable and I said I didn't know, so he said something like "I'm beginning to think you've got a secret lover" and I said "Yes I have".'

'To which he said what?'

'He laughed, and patted me on the bottom. He thought I was joking too.'

William ruminated fleetingly on Rosemary's sanity. His relief was such that he could not be angry. He felt even like smiling, but decided that it would not be seemly.

'So in other words all this was a trick to persuade me to meet you?'

Rosemary nodded glumly, her face filling effortlessly with self-pity.

'I didn't know how else I could see you. Robin's making me go on holiday soon and I wanted to find out if we could arrange anything about Bristol for next weekend.'

'I can't go to Bristol, Rosemary. You know that.'

'You said you would.'

'I said I'd like to and that I'd try, and then I told you I *had* tried and I couldn't.'

'You said you'd definitely go.'

'And now I'm telling you that I definitely can't.'

'What about Pringle's flat, then? Aren't you going to take me there any more?'

'If I was taking you anywhere, which since you've raised the question I'm not, the last place would be Pringle's flat,' retorted William.

'Because you're nervous of going?'

'Because you had an affair with him and won't admit it. And because I don't see why I should waste my time with a bloody liar.'

Rosemary did not respond to this. She had not stopped looking down at her thumbs and her voice had not risen above a sullen monotone. There was, William could tell from these signs, more to come. The fiction about her husband had only been an exercise in psychological warfare: a leaflet raid demanding unconditional surrender. Now, in sorrow not in anger, she was priming the high explosive. She would resume in a moment in a low voice, with a statement so oblique that William would not be able to challenge it, ignore it or shrug it off. He would be forced to cross-examine her until his curiosity was satisfied. Slowly she would allow him to drag out of her a confession so awful that it would leave him bemused like the victim of an accident. Subsequently he would spend many unhappy hours pottering around in a landslide of facts, gradually piecing together a completely new conception of Rosemary in the light of the bizarre information she had thrown at him. This, he knew, was her infallible way of retaining her interest. He often wondered what masochistic trait made his response so predictable.

Rosemary said:

'I know I lie to you sometimes but part of what I told you was true. About there being somebody else.'

'You mean what you told Robin?'

'No. What I'm telling you now.'

'I see. You want to tell me about Pringle?'

'You know about Pringle already. The only reason I went with him was because you wouldn't find a place where we could make love. I thought you didn't want me.'

'Leaving that aside for the moment, you mean there's been someone else besides Pringle?'

'Yes.'

'Who?'

'A man.'

'I've already grasped that. Which man?'

'Somebody at the office.'

'When?'

'The other day, after we had that row about Pringle. I was feeling unhappy and wretched – you hadn't rung me and I didn't know what you were thinking about me. This man took me for a drink. Then he gave me a lift home. Robin was at work. So ...' Here Rosemary shrugged, suggesting that making love to a man from the office was the completely natural consequence to her husband's absence.

William made a token effort to do something about the alarming pains in his chest which he diagnosed as pangs of jealousy. He told himself that Rosemary's movements were of no further interest to him. He thought of mentioning his own adventure with Jackie by way of revenge. He tried to visualize the bedroom in Marylebone Lane so that he could recall some hurtful titbit. But he had difficulty in keeping Jackie's face in his mind and after a few seconds it faded away, leaving only the firm impression of her mouth, like the Cheshire Cat's grin in *Alice*. This ample crescent served as a frame for a clear picture of Rosemary – who had once sworn to him that he was the only man with whom she was not totally frigid – sprawled on the floor with a man from the office.

'Has this happened before? I mean besides Pringle and this other man?'

'It always happens.'

'What do you mean, it "always" happens?'

'Every time I think you don't want me.'

'And how often has that been?'

'Too often.'

'Three times? Four times?'

'More than that.'

'Come along, Rosemary. I want to know how many.'

'Do you mean times, or people?'

'You know perfectly well what I mean. How many other men have there been while you've been going about with me?'

'I don't know. Eleven, I think.'

24

One of his preoccupations was a nagging consciousness that he had nothing to think about. It troubled him most in the late evening when television was about to finish: he had a compound memory of long dead hours spent lounging in armchairs or lying in bed with his eyes open, feeling nothing, contemplating nothing, his mind so under-worked that it registered the clicking of the electricity meter in the hall, and every random sound.

He had long ago analysed this deficiency. He was not industrious enough to channel his thoughts towards work outside business hours, nor ambitious enough to be able to relax in dreams of a prosperous retirement. He had no particular beliefs, and so could not turn to pious thoughts. Family matters upset him too much for him to dwell on them at length. Occasionally he indulged himself in erotic fantasies about Rosemary, and lately about Jackie, but these soon palled, and in any case they were so over-laden with anxiety and guilt that he was glad to shut them off. His most pleasurable thinking was to do with small, concrete luxuries: a new tube of toothpaste to be opened, the great alleviation of not needing a haircut for another two weeks, and Sunday papers waiting on the doorstep. There was a vacancy in his mind that in a more secure age might have been filled by the contemplation of rewarding hobbies such as cycling or philately, in a less secure one by the fear of bombs or by the persuasions of some colourful political party. To fill the void William would often consciously exhume some period of his life – his schooldays, or his R AF career – and carefully chew the meat off these bones, sometimes deliberately keeping back a morsel of incident – dormitory evenings, the friendly mess dinners – to sustain him another day.

He did not want to think about Rosemary's eleven lovers. He knew that he was emotionally unequipped for it. But as the evening wore on, television ran itself down into the small-talk of parliamentary debate and epilogues, he laid his book aside and began to brood on the classical elements of jealousy, betrayal and deceit with which he was enmeshed. With little else to occupy his mind it was not long before he began to warm towards the role of the Othello of Tulip Street.

The concept of Rosemary's eleven lovers was abstract in its enormity. The main task was to establish it on a statistical basis by visualizing eleven actual men. In deference to Rosemary's background – she was quite well educated, and her father had been a lieutenant-colonel in a Guards regiment – William saw them first of all in dinner jackets, falling rather drunkenly out of the Dorchester after a reunion of some kind and piling into taxis. This for a while was a sharp enough image, and he dwelt for a time on the picture of three cabloads of lovers careering for some reason round and round Piccadilly Circus. But the unequal distribution of passengers – four lovers in each of the first two taxis but only three in the last – upset William's sense of symmetry. He let the taxis vanish into the fog of his sub-conscious and then, lethargically, allowed various pictures of virile masculinity in combinations of eleven to pass through his mind. He saw an Air Force bomber crew, a bus queue, a town council, a jury (with one absentee), the personnel of a small factory, a dance band, a row of bowler-hatted stencil-men on a productivity chart. In one image – he acknowledged the phallic symbolism – he saw an execution squad of eleven soldiers, firing bullets at the blindfold figure of Rosemary. He saw a posse of Sicilian bandits, and a television camera team. At length (he was not interested in sport, or it would have occurred to him earlier) he saw a cricket team, and he quickly recognized this as the image he was looking for. Hanging on a wall of the Bucket Shop, between a Victorian sampler and a commemorative plate bearing a picture of John Wesley, was an old sepia photograph of the Surrey Cricket Eleven for 1885. The captain, sporting W. G. Grace whiskers and holding a bat between his knees, sat on a hard chair in the centre of the group, while two others were draped on the grass on either side of him, chins cupped in their hands. The rest, ranging from the centre according to size, stood in two stolid lines behind. All had moustaches. William saw Rosemary in a long tulle dress and picture hat, wandering to the pavilion during the tea interval and being systematically and repeatedly deflowered after strawberries and cream.

But not even this piquant vision did justice to Rosemary's revelations.

'How many lovers have you really had?' William had asked her finally.

'I've told you – eleven.'

'I mean in all.'

'Since I met you?'

'You mean there've been others since you met me?'

'There was one when we had that stupid quarrel at Christmas, over you not turning up for a drink. And one when you went off on holiday with Poodle last year. But I told you about them.'

'No you didn't, you only said you'd been for a meal with one and a drink with the other.'

'And then I told you that one of them took me home, and the other asked me back to his place.'

'Ignoring that for the time being, how many altogether?'

'Counting those two?'

'Counting everybody. Altogether.'

'What – *all* together? Since I was born?'

'Yes.'

'I don't know. A lot.'

Before William fell asleep the memory of a fragment of wartime newsreel flashed into his mind. A battalion of the Kings Own Yorkshire Light Infantry was leaving for the front. Shouldering kitbags and rifles, an endless line of fresh-faced conscripts stamped up the gang-plank of a troopship, grinning broadly and raising cocky thumbs to the cameras of British Movietone News. This was a fully satisfying piece of imagery and it occupied his mind intermittently for forty-eight hours, when some thoughts about Jackie began to intrude.

25

The Oxford Junior Encyclopaedia, which William had bought for Melisande on her ninth birthday in the slender hope of stimulating her mind, contained nothing about venereal diseases. There was no other encyclopedia in the house. There were very few books of any kind apart from a vast paperback collection of horse stories that seemed exclusively to form Melisande's literary diet. William owned several popular guides to porcelain, old silver and antique furniture from which he had hoped to learn the mysteries of his trade, and very occasionally he bought a volume of popular sociology or an exposé of some political scandal in which his interest had been temporarily inflamed by the Sunday newspapers. He never read novels. Poodle never seemed to read anything at all.

He began to worry about his social health after a conversation with Pringle.

'Rent, please!'

'Spent, thank you!' said William, imagining that he was riposting to some piece of facetiousness.

'Seriously though, I could use it,' said Pringle. 'Nine pounds, I think you owe me.'

'For what?'

'If you've forgotten, we agreed that you'd pay four-ten a week for borrowing my room. That was two weeks ago, so I make it nine quid.'

'But I've only been there once!'

'Yes, but we didn't really go into how often you were going to use it, did we? The room's there, any time you want it. It's up to you.'

'And another thing,' said William. 'I don't think I shall be using it again.'

'Ah, well that puts me somewhat in shtuck, unfortunately. You see, when you asked me for the room I was on the point of getting somebody to share the rent because quite frankly I can't pay it all myself. And when you offered to chip in I did actually turn down a bloke I'd been dickering with. I thought I could rely on your share for three months at least, just till we get *Lost* off the ground.'

'That's a bit awkward,' said William.

'Yes, it is a bit awkward.'

'I rather got the impression when you asked me to invest in the play that you were, well, lending me the flat for nothing.'

'We're not millionaires yet,' said Pringle. And it was as he pocketed nine pound notes from William's till that he added: 'There's one good thing. If you've not been using the place it signifies, I hope and trust, that you've not been going through Jackie Douglas.'

William, forgetting his grievance over the rent, bracketed this statement with Pringle's earlier warning about Rosemary.

'Why do you say that – is she trouble?' He felt masochistic pride in seeing himself through Pringle's eyes as a human lemming perpetually entangled with neurotic women.

'A mate of mine very strongly suspects that she gave him a dose last year. He could be wrong, or alternatively she might have had herself seen to by now.'

'A dose?'

'And I don't mean cough medicine, either.'

'I don't believe it,' said William positively, hoping that Pringle would then laugh, wink, shrug or otherwise mitigate his almost paralytic feeling of terror.

'So you have been there? Any interesting symptoms?'

'What kind of symptoms?'

'Morning drip? Red end? Outhouse trots?'

This expertise was new to William but he had not the courage to ask for a translation.

'No. Nothing of that kind.'

'You're not for instance dashing off for a pee every five minutes?'

'No.' He immediately had a strong desire to go to the lavatory.

'She's had herself seen to, then. But I'm not joking. She almost definitely had a dose and this mate of mine got it, to name only one. It was like bloody *La Ronde* with her at one time.'

He took to examining himself in the bathroom several times a day. At first he noticed nothing alarming but after he had bought a torch in Woolworth's he became aware of certain physical peculiarities that might or might not have been present before his encounter with Jackie. Prolonged inspection brought to light several distressing symptoms that could conceivably be defined by the technical expressions used by Pringle. William told himself that they were probably psychosomatic and that if he turned his mind to other matters they would go away. He began to go through the Bucket Shop's annual accounts with the idea, based on a principle of ancient Chinese medicine, of removing one worry by the substitution of another. But his scrutiny of the depressing figures was interrupted so constantly by urgent visits to the lavatory that at the end of the day he was well on the way to persuading himself that he was a syphilitic bankrupt. He closed his account books wearily and took himself to Fulham Reference Library, where he consulted the *Encyclopaedia Britannica*. He learned that if he was not suffering from primary syphilis he had almost certainly contracted chancroid, a disease normally restricted to tropical areas. After the first shock a reaction of dull fatalism set in and William was comparatively encouraged, upon turning to Black's Medical Dictionary, to learn that at worst prolonged disability and tissue destruction might ensue.

In what perspective he could manage he tried to see his predicament from a moral rather than a medical viewpoint. He thought about Jackie, and about Rosemary, and condemned them both. If Rosemary hadn't been promiscuous he would never have turned to Jackie. On the other hand Jackie must have been equally promiscuous to have – the words came to him from an enamelled notice in a public urinal: 'incurred infection.' But there was to be said for Jackie that she had not pretended to be anything she was not and that she did live in a world where promiscuity was the norm. But then there was to be said for Rosemary that as far as she was concerned promiscuity was *not* the norm, and she was not so depraved that it was no longer a burning issue between them. On the other hand Jackie had not used her own degeneracy as an emotional weapon against him. At the same time Rosemary did have the elementary wit to safeguard her health if not her virtue.

The debate concluded without a vote being taken. William decided to have nothing more to do with either of them and went to see his doctor.

26

Poodle was mistaken in believing that she had established a pattern of communication with Pringle. Although she loitered frequently outside his flat he did not whistle for her again. She telephoned him several times but he was not in, or did not answer. She sent him several notes which yielded no response. Yesterday while she did her morning sentry-go outside his home he had emerged at high speed and jumped into a radio cab.

Consequently Poodle was in a bad temper at breakfast when William told her that he had to go along to a hospital near London Bridge for a check-up.

'But it's Melisande's half-holiday. I thought you were going to have a day off from the shop today and take her up the GPO Tower or somewhere?'

'I can only do what the doctor tells me to do. I *am* having a day off, but I do have to go to this wretched hospital.'

'And what check-up? You don't go to hospital for a check-up. I thought your own doctor was supposed to give you a check-up.'

The repetition of 'check-up' made William's story sound thin, as it was intended to do. Poodle proposed to spend most of the day laying siege for Pringle. She did not doubt that William was going where he said he was going but true to her policy she saw no reason why he should not be accompanied by an uneasy conscience.

From his own point of view William thought it judicious to elaborate his story.

'It's not really a check-up – he wants me to have an X-ray.'

'Why? You haven't got TB.'

'No, but I've been having these pains down here and he wants to make sure I don't have a stone in my kidneys.'

'If you had a stone in your kidneys you'd surely know about it.'

'That's for the doctor to say.'

'And why do you have to go trailing off to London Bridge? There's a hospital only down the road – haven't *they* got an X-ray unit?'

'Possibly so, but apparently I've got to see this specialist.'

Poodle felt almost sorry for William: it was so easy to get him flustered.

'I wish you'd make your mind up. First you're going for a check-up, then it's an X-ray, and now you say you're. . .'

William was sweating with the effort and embarrassment of lying his way out of the house. It was in his favour that he looked and felt ill. It was now Friday and he had not slept properly since Tuesday, when his doctor refused to give him the all-clear he had been praying for and insisted on dispatching him to a clinic. It was, so the doctor said, only a formality – certain tests would be made and then William's mind would be put completely at rest. If he thought this was reassuring the doctor reckoned without the resilience of William's anxiety neurosis which, with the same survival technique as an amoeba, immediately split itself in two. His original fear of infection was now supplemented by a fear of what would happen to him at the clinic – he had heard some horrifying stories in his RAF days – and whether he would be able to stand the treatment if his suspicions were confirmed.

These preoccupations, since Tuesday, had jostled for precedence in his mind, either one constantly replacing and replenishing the other. During the night, however, there had been a further molecular change in the structure of his anxieties, when he began to ponder on the enormous question of keeping the whole sordid business a secret from Poodle. Since the early hours he had been wrestling with the most immediate aspect of this problem, which was how to account for his absence from the Bucket Shop today.

He made up his mind first to pretend that he was going to a sale of furniture in the country; but at the low metabolism hour of four in the morning this seemed too dangerously simple to be convincing. What if she found out where he had really been? His impression of hospital procedure was of white cards fluttering through the letter box, confirming appointments made; while he believed they were discreet at these places it would be obvious to Poodle that he was having medical attention of some kind, and she would wonder why he had been so secretive. It was best to be half-honest. Various excuses for visiting a hospital recommended themselves to him: a suspected ulcer, an impacted wisdom tooth, a slipped disc, a urine test, – he rejected this as being too clever by half – a blood test, an eye test. The eye test seemed his best proposition, for he was in fact troubled by short-sightedness, and in the interests of verisimilitude he was working out a fictitious encounter with student doctors at the Ophthalmic Clinic when suddenly his ever-vigilant fears changed shape and joined together again, and he remembered vividly what the *Encyclopaedia Britannica* had said on the theme of blindness as a result of tertiary syphilis.

He reached the breakfast table haggard and confused, with no clear alibi in his mind, and he had begun mumbling about a check-up in the pathetic hope that Poodle would not question him too deeply about it.

He interrupted her:

'I don't know why you're being so difficult about it. I have for once in my life got to go to the hospital. Whether it's for a check-up or an X-ray or to see a specialist is beside the point. Surely I can be allowed to go with the minimum of fuss.'

Melisande had meanwhile come down to breakfast. She was always the last at table: if William had not been so concerned with his own health he would have urged Poodle to take her to the doctor and find out why she was never to be found shovelling cornflakes inside herself like the happy, inquisitive children one saw in television commercials.

'Daddy, instead of going to the BBC Tower can we go to Peppin Forest?'

'It's not the BBC Tower, it's the GPO Tower, and it's not Peppin Forest, it's Epping Forest. You know that perfectly well, or ought to.'

'Well, can we go to Pepping Forest?'

'*Epping* Forest.'

'Epping Forest.'

'We can't go to Epping Forest, chum, no,' said William. 'Daddy's not very well, and I have to go to hospital for an X-ray.'

'Can I come with you?'

'Of course you can't!'

'But what do you imagine she's going to do all day?' said Poodle. 'I've got to go out, all her friends are going away for the half-holiday, and you did promise to take her out today.'

'You did promise, daddy, and what do you 'magine I'm going to *do* all day?'

'William? Surely she can sit in the waiting room – they won't keep you all morning.'

'I can take a comic to read,' said Melisande.

'But they don't encourage children in these places,' protested William. It was a weak reply but he felt desperately sick. He wished now that he'd said he was going to see a psychiatrist about a probable nervous breakdown, for he felt he was on the verge of one.

'Nonsense. You see babies in *prams* in hospital waiting rooms. Anyway, she's never been to a hospital before. She'd like it.'

'I'd like it, daddy. I've never been to a hostipal before.'

'Hospital.'

'Hospital.'

'She'd better go to the lavatory before you set off,' said Poodle.

William, who wanted to go to the lavatory himself for the fourth time that morning, felt too ill to argue further. As a result, when he reported later that morning to the Venereal Disease Clinic near London Bridge, his nine-year-old daughter accompanied him. Fortunately the clinic was housed in a general hospital; Melisande was not a curious child and she asked no questions when her father, after a muttered conversation with an attendant, left her in the lobby while he slunk off to a nissen hut in the hospital grounds.

27

William had read, or thought he had read, that the treatment of social diseases was now enlightened and that those seeking prompt treatment need have no fear of being humiliated. This did not seem to be true. He was questioned offensively by a man he thought was a doctor but who later was identified as an orderly.

'And I suppose you don't know the name and address of the contact?'

'Yes, since you ask me, I do,' said William with spirit. He thought the fact might put him in a separate class from other patients (of whom none was visible) and that he might be given more sensitive attention.

But the orderly did not seem impressed.

'I'll tell you what to do about that later. Come with me.'

He was taken before a white-coated doctor who did not look up from his papers or address him directly. Various tests were taken, most of them with litmus paper as if he were the subject of an experiment at school, and then he was conducted to a small cubicle where he was left to ponder his fate.

William supposed that many people must have sat where he

sat now and that they must have reflected on the circumstances which had brought them there. His own wrong turnings were so numerous that it was difficult to trace his present situation to any definite source. He resumed, or rather recapitulated, his moral debate. If only Rosemary had not confessed to having an affair with Pringle, he would not have taken Jackie to dinner, or to bed. But if only he had been more self-contained he would have had no need of Rosemary, or of Jackie either. If he had kept out of Kemble's Club he would never have met Jackie. If Pringle had not interested him in *Lost* he would never have gone to Kemble's Club. If he had never opened the Bucket Shop he would not have met Pringle. If only he had authenticated himself as a qualified antique dealer he would be in Bond Street by now and would never have opened the Bucket Shop.

Compulsively, remove by remove, he edged backwards through his career until he found himself at the familiar cliff-edge of his own adequacy. He tried different routes – if only Poodle had been a more successful wife, if only he had not married her, if only he had not met her – but, however tortuously, he was led back to the same dismal prospect.

Time passed slowly. The cubicle was claustrophobic. There was nothing to read except some files on a small table, and he was afraid to open them. There seemed to be no real view from the window but he went to it and by craning his neck towards an eyeline of about fifteen degrees he was able to look out. He saw a tree, a coke compound, a stack of empty oxygen cylinders and a girl, too tall for her age, in an unsuitable pink dress. Melisande was wandering, at the moment, quite aimlessly about the hospital grounds; but there was only one positive route she could eventually take and that was in the direction of the nissen hut clinic. She walked round in faltering circles and William could tell from the droop of her shoulders that she was about to start crying if she was not doing so already. She finally determined her steps towards the asphalt path leading to the nissen hut, and she must have been within reading distance of the sign that said 'SPECIAL CLINIC' before a nurse ran after her and conducted her back to the main building.

William had been alone in the cubicle for an hour. He went into the small reception office where the orderly was drinking coffee.

'I wonder if you could tell me how long I shall have to wait?'

'No idea.'

'You see, my daughter is waiting for me outside and . . .'

'Your *what*?'

'My daughter.'

'How old is she?' The orderly, as a reflex action against any untoward circumstance, had picked up a ballpoint pen and drawn some official sheet of paper before him. Blind fear seized William.

'You don't have to know that, surely?'

The orderly gave him a curious look and walked out of the office. In a moment he returned and told William that the doctor was ready for him.

'You'll be pleased to hear that the tests are negative.'

'And that means . . .?'

'That there's nothing whatsoever wrong with you. Or I should say at least there's nothing wrong with the tools of your trade.'

William acknowledged the small crudity with a faint smile. As if observing someone else he registered his own response. He did not feel relief yet, only a vague consciousness of his ability to smile – the slowly-developing awareness of someone who has been paralyzed.

The doctor had earlier asked him to sit and he thought he would now take up this invitation. He sat down slowly and luxuriously, able to feel the life in each limb and so sensuously appreciative of the blood flowing in his body that he had the sensation of eating ripe fruit. He began to breathe, taking long, slow draughts of air not from necessity but for the taste. He leaned back in his chair, and from the pleasurable minutiae of his reactions he selected the unlikeliest one, which was that what he could do with now was a long glass of his mother's home-made lemonade.

The doctor said:

'I imagine you've had a very worrying week of it.'

'Very.'

'I'm giving you a note to your own doctor. He might want to prescribe a mild sedative. I should think you're feeling pretty bunched-up, aren't you?'

'Bunched-up?'

'Tense. Things crowding in on you. A tight feeling in the chest – do you get that?'

'Yes, I do.' William felt a new respect for the doctor whom, in this nissen hut outpost, he had hitherto pigeon-holed as a semi-outcast from professional life, like a remittance man in a story by Somerset Maugham.

'These symptoms that have been bothering you are probably the result of anxiety. You may have heard of people who worry about cancer, for example – they start looking for signs, prodding themselves and so forth, and nature obliges with all sorts of aches and pains and bumps.'

'Yes, I have heard that,' said William warily. As the first flush of well-being passed he was beginning to feel slightly foolish.

'Let me ask you this. You're not – you won't mind my putting it in this fashion – what you'd call a promiscuous man as a rule?'

'Er – no.'

'What led to these symptoms was, shall we say, an isolated incident?'

'I suppose so.'

'And it rather bothered you? Made you feel guilty to some extent?'

'To some extent.'

The doctor swivelled in his chair and pushed his spectacles up over his forehead. He had no more patients and had nothing to do until lunchtime.

'I don't know what's in your mind as a result of this scare but I think you'd be very well advised to think over very carefully any ideas you might have about leading anything in the nature of a double life.' Without giving William time to fillet the qualifications from this the doctor continued: 'I'm not preaching morals at you, that's not my job – it's simply a question of temperament. You're either cut out for that kind of life or you're not. It's like being a politician or a racing driver or a heavyweight boxer – wanting the rewards isn't enough, you've got to be prepared for the risks and indeed you've got to *welcome* the risks – you've got to want that kind of life because it's the only kind of life you're capable of leading. Now if you try to follow a social pattern that's alien to you it's going to set up all sorts of tensions. You'll be leading at best a mildly schizophrenic existence and you may finish up in a far worse state, mentally speaking that is, than you thought you were in when you came to see me this morning. I'm not trying to say that you shouldn't enjoy yourself and as I say, God forbid that I should try and preach to you, but because some of your friends may be able to get away with all sorts of things it doesn't necessarily mean that you are the kind of person who can. Does that make any sense to you?'

'I think so,' said William.

The doctor was anxious to get all that he had said written down, for he had just decided to write a popular book about success and the sex impulse. He got up and shook William's hand, and wished him good luck.

28

In the main lobby of the hospital, convinced that her father had been taken off for a serious operation and that she would soon be pitched into the busy street to find her own way home, Melisande bit her lip and blinked back tears. Although William would never see it, she had inherited many of his characteristics, and one of them was a tendency to luxuriate in worry. She was also introspective, cautious, insecure, and an escapist. Her aim in life had always been to become a groom in a riding school, but now, imagining her father being conveyed out of the operating theatre with a sheet over his head, she was able to derive a measure of comfort from seeing herself as the nurse detailed to wheel him to the mortuary.

Melisande was not as stupid as William thought her: she had reserves of intelligence on which, since she shared his lack of ambition, she had never found it necessary to draw. She learned things when she wanted to please her parents or her teachers, and declined to learn them when she wanted to please herself. By and large this meant that Melisande was likely to become a reasonably educated person, for she set great store by giving happiness of a sentimental kind to others. She preferred to give rather than to receive, not from motives of selflessness but because the act of giving removed the social burden of gratitude to other shoulders. In this, she perhaps took after Poodle rather than William.

She had developed lately the habit of finding small sums of money: a half crown that she was nearly sure belonged to her; a shilling (from a girl's desk at school) that might be the one she had mislaid last term; a florin (in the recesses of an armchair) that had not necessarily fallen out of her father's pocket. With these funds she always intended to buy gifts for her parents. Their pleasure would be delightful: they would be touched by her thoughtfulness and would not be able to bring themselves to criticize her grammar or her manners or her eating habits. But when Melisande went to the shops the gifts she had in mind were always too expensive and she bought sweets for herself instead, resolving half-heartedly to save but knowing that she had not the strength of mind to amass the fifteen or twenty shillings needed for a stationery set or a pot of flowers. She had William's gift for candid self-assessment.

Her personal happiness was derived from reading pony books. She was not particularly interested in horses and skipped the passages describing the actual riding and jumping: but in all these books there was a recurring passage where the palomino or chestnut was led back to the stables to be rubbed down; cold evening came; there was a scrubbed kitchen crowded with children, parents, cousins, young aunts and dogs; there were home-made scones (which she had never eaten), pears from the garden, honey, brown bread, jugs of milk, and all this was followed by a scraping of chairs on the brick floor, a lighting of pipes by the uncles and a babble of voices from which emerged a firm cry of: 'This calls for a Family Conference!'

The discrepancy between this and her own existence in Tulip

Street did not worry Melisande. She would have been interested to hear that William endorsed her fantasies in principle and she might have offered to lend him one of her pony books. But she accepted that her own life was of a mundane sort, that home-made scones belonged to another generation if not to another race of people, and that even if her parents were to respond to a cry of 'Let's have a Family Conference!' they, and she, would be only play-acting. In this respect, at least, Melisande differed from her father.

The only vicarious element in her reading that was carried forward into reality was a faithful reproduction of warm excitement when William promised her some treat or other. The actual event – a visit to the theatre, an outing to Battersea Fun Fair – was usually a disappointment, but in looking forward to it Melisande had the great pleasure of identifying with some scene or other in one of her books. In the re-creation of such a scene she usually found it necessary to call up an imaginary cousin, nanny or sister: 'Papa has promised that if we're good he might take us to the zoo tomorrow.' – 'O! And will there be giraffes, and monkeys, and buns for the elephants?' These indulgences were inspired by older volumes than her pony books; Melisande knew instinctively that the family treat, as a completely redeemable pledge, was buried even deeper in mythology than the family conference in the brick kitchen of Orchard Farm. But she was always bitterly disappointed when William went back on his word; she cried, went to her room and read pony books.

William was beaming with pleasure when he returned to the hospital lobby. Melisande was not used to any demonstration of affection from her father, so that when he tried to hug her she was taken off-balance. Propelled backwards along the parquet floor she grabbed at a stationary invalid chair. It skidded away from her and she fell on a wastepaper basket, scraping her elbow. She tried not to cry, knowing that William would become bad-tempered, but she could not stop tears of pain welling up in her eyes. To her surprise William was genuinely apologetic. He kissed the place to make it better and then took her to a Wimpy Bar for lunch, holding her hand all the way.

'Can I have a Coca-Cola instead of milk, daddy?'

'Of course you can, darling.'

Deeply suspicious of her father's geniality, Melisande made a test case of picking the onions out of her hamburger, a practice usually certain to infuriate him.

All William said was: 'And where would you like to go this afternoon – the BBC Tower or Pepping Forest?'

'The forest,' replied Melisande carefully, suspecting sarcasm.

'Pepping Forest or Epping Forest?'

'Epping Forest.'

The outing was a qualified success. William was able without difficulty to capture and re-capture the sensation of voluptuous ease which had flooded over him at the clinic. It was the first feeling of any substance that he had experienced since Rosemary told him about her eleven lovers, and he indulged himself to the hilt. He felt like a man who had just been released from prison. In Epping Forest he breathed in the scent of ferns, sniffed the flowers and the berries, listened to the sound of birds, and was only put out when he began to realize that he could not identify any single one of them. Nor could Melisande, and William could not stop himself from becoming mildly irritated with her.

'What's that tree there?'

'I think it's an oak, daddy.'

'Everything's a blessed oak according to you. Don't you have nature study at school?'

'Sometimes.'

'Then surely you know that an oak has sort of crinkly leaves. Now this tree doesn't have crinkly leaves, does it?'

'No, daddy.'

'Then it can't be an oak, can it?'

But this slight ill-humour did not last for long. He led his daughter deep into the forest, encouraging her to gather flowers that neither of them knew the names of. He did not envy the occasional young couples who crossed his path on their way to some private shrubbery, and did not even recall that he had once escorted Rosemary in the same direction, and with the same peculiar gait – a purposeful route march wearing the camouflage of an afternoon stroll.

Melisande found something on the ground.

'Is this a horse-chestnut, daddy?'

'I'm not sure.'

'Can I eat it?'

'I don't know. I shouldn't.'

It slightly disturbed him that neither of them was equipped to enjoy their expedition to the full. On the way to the forest by Central Line he had seen himself pointing with a stick at various plants with picturesque names like Old Mother's Whiskers and Milkmaids-a-Courting. He would tell Melisande amusing stories about how they had got these names, and she would scamper about gathering specimens to press into an album. Instead, they seemed to be standing aimlessly in the middle of a path, gazing at what could be a horse chestnut or, for all he knew, a mildewed golf ball.

He wondered what he could do about it. He had seen some little books in W. H. Smith's – *British Birds, British Trees, British Flowers* and so on; he would buy them and learn to identify one bird and one tree every day. There would be more outings to the forest, and to Windsor Great Park and Whipsnade.

William suddenly wished that he had a son. They could sail boats on the Round Pond, fly kites, go fishing, and breed white mice that would escape and frighten Poodle.

In the meantime, there was always Melisande.

'Look, daddy, a little animal!'

'I don't see anything.'

'There! Look!'

'Oh, yes. I wonder what it is.'

29

'We are having an evening out, after all. I do wish you could pick another topic of conversation.'

'She is your daughter, William.'

'Yes, I know that. I did take her to Epping Forest the other day and I did spend half last evening doing a jigsaw with her. Now I'd like to enjoy my meal.'

'But aren't you worried about her?'

'To tell you the truth, what worries me at the moment is whether the waiter heard me ask for spinach.'

They were in a Greek restaurant recommended by *Queen* magazine. It was not often that William took Poodle out to dinner, and she was being tiresome. There had been some unpleasantness at Melisande's school – petty thefts in the cloakroom, and the loss of a purse containing seven shillings. William didn't see why, if the subject had to be discussed at all, it couldn't be discussed at home.

'William? I know Melisande wouldn't steal anything but she does seem to have a knack of finding things, and I've been wondering if possibly half a crown might have rolled out of somebody's coat and she's . . .'

'Possibly. I do think plastic cruets rather let this place down, don't you?'

'And she always seems to have money these days, half crowns and two shilling pieces. Who gives it to her?'

'I do, very often. So do you. Is this melon ripe, would you say?'

'No, but it's not one of their specialities. I don't see how we can say anything.'

'Perhaps not.'

'And William, what you've got to remember is that when you give her money or I give her money she immediately goes off and buys sweets and things, but she always seems to have a fortune left over.'

'That's because she comes home with cheap rubbish. You let her buy these penny licorice sticks and everlasting toffee and God knows what else they sell at that corner shop, and then you wonder why she's always down with stomach ache.'

William tried to steer the talk back to the food, the service and the décor. He was determined to have a social evening with his wife. He drew Poodle's attention to a Turkish coffee pot that was very similar to one he had once nearly sold to a Canadian woman, and gave her a précis of a book review he had scanned in the paper that morning. He remarked that Poodle and he did not dine out often enough. He reminded her of the small bistro where they sometimes used to share a table with friends before they were married, and suggested that one of these days they ought to make up a foursome and find some interesting restaurant in Soho. But neither of them could think of any friends with whom they were still in touch. The conversation lapsed, and the meal continued in silence.

Idly scanning the menu and looking at the tables on either side of him William recognized the same vague discontent as he had felt on his outing with Melisande a few days earlier. The people at the next table were eating with relish some kind of pâté which they shovelled into their mouths with flat hot cakes of Greek bread; on the other side a party of four were attacking what he supposed were kebabs or shashliks of some kind, with a salad of chopped peppers and something baked in vine leaves. William envied their gusto but knew that he had been wise to choose a fillet steak and that Poodle was being as adventurous as it was reasonable to expect in asking for American fried chicken. The rough Greek wine would not suit them and so he'd ordered Beaujolais. A waiter, presumably sensing his illiterate palate, offered him a miniature loaf of Hovis from a basket instead of the primitive hot baps that his neighbours were enjoying. William felt, as he sometimes did, that he was leading a diluted life. He would put the *Good Food Guide* on his list of recommended reading, along with *British Birds* and *British Trees*.

These musings apart, he was feeling reasonably pleased with himself. That morning Pringle had dropped in at the Bucket Shop and during negotiations concerning an ancient wooden half-plate camera that took his fancy he had agreed, conditional on having the camera for nothing, to release William from his rental agreement. Knowing that William had entered his flat only once in a sub-tenancy of several weeks, Pringle remarked jocularly that he would have found it cheaper with a Park Lane whore. The talk led naturally to the subject of Jackie, to whom William gave a clean bill of health, and then to Rosemary. He found himself asking diffidently what Pringle thought about her as a lover.

'Bloody awful,' said Pringle. This opinion cheered William enormously. It salved wounded pride and restored his confidence in his own prowess. He was also gratified to learn that there was seemingly no great market for what he had rejected himself. He felt that he had shown great judgement in deciding to settle down with Poodle again.

'Does your wife know you've been having it away with Randy Rosemary?' asked Pringle.

'I sincerely hope not.'

There was a pause before Pringle spoke again. It was not often in his dialogues with William that he took the diffident role.

'Does she go in for it herself?'

'Who? What?'

'Your wife. Does she ever have it on the side, to the best of your knowledge?'

'Good God, no!'

But the notion that Poodle might have been unfaithful was for a reason he could not comprehend the most erotic one to enter his mind for some time. It stayed with him all day, inspired him to invite her out to the Greek restaurant for dinner, and encouraged him – when, after a meal conducted for three quarters of its duration in silence, they got home again – to make love to her with a fervour which astounded them both. The following day Poodle was civil to him for the first time in weeks and in the evening they tried to repeat the essay. But the mood had by then gone for both of them, and the experiment failed.

30

Several weeks passed in tranquillity. Rosemary telephoned him
once more; he hung up on her. Now she was going on holiday
and after that she would be touring the provinces for her
magazine, doubtless going to bed with its various regional
representatives. He had lost Jackie's number, or rather thrown
it away – he discovered her scrawled cigarette packet in his
wallet when, in Epping Forest with Melisande, he took out
and read the note to his doctor from the London Bridge clinic.
He tore up both documents and dropped them in the hollow
stump of what was possibly an oak tree.

His business ticked over satisfactorily. He took Melisande
once to Hyde Park and once to the Royal Tournament, when
they left in the interval because she was sick. He made elaborate arrangements for a picnic but it was rained off and they
went to a news theatre instead. He began to smoke a pipe. He
got home early in the evenings and spent them reading *The
Forsyte Saga* in the Penguin edition. The only flaw in his arrangements was that these days Poodle was perpetually in a
bad mood. He identified himself with Soames and made the
best of it.

31

It was not often that Poodle came into the Bucket Shop. William had always hoped that after Melisande had settled down
at school his wife would help him run the business. There was
always an excuse: she was too busy in the house, she could not
see herself haggling with stray American tourists. If William
was persistent she told the truth: that she thought he was a
glorified market trader and that the Bucket Shop – he had
over-bought recently on a job lot of wax fruit and a consign-
ment of cast-iron pineapples – put her in mind of a petrified
fruit stall. But sometimes she called in with a piece of bric-à-

brac that one of the mothers at school had asked her to get rid of, or to see if there was anything in the shop worth having for the house in Tulip Street.

'Those prints have been stuck up there rather a long time, haven't they?'

'They're not prints, they're lithographs.'

'What's the difference?'

'It's too complicated to explain.'

'You mean someone sold them to you and told you they were lithographs.'

William knew of shops that were run by husband-and-wife teams who stimulated and fortified each other and supplemented each other's knowledge: the husband, a specialist in silver, would come home with a little painted thimble thrown in with a collection of Georgian snuff-boxes; the wife, bright as a button, would identify it as Bilston enamel. William wished Poodle would take a more intelligent interest in his business – for one thing, he could not afford a paid assistant.

'What I'm looking for,' said Poodle after taking a deprecatory inventory of the stock, 'is something that would make a good door-stop for the hall. One of those iron pineapple things might do.'

'Those happen to be in sets of six. They're Regency bosses from the stair-rails of a Nash terrace.'

'Nonsense, they've been sawn off the railings round Battersea Park.'

'Anyway, you can't have one. Look in the workshop and see if there's a flat iron or a kitchen weight or something.'

The workshop was a basement room where William had laid in supplies of gold leaf, mahogany veneer and glue against the day when he would be competent enough to engage in the craft of restoring antique furniture. He had not yet acquired the necessary skills, the basement had become partly-flooded, and the workshop was now a depository for items which he had lost hope of selling.

As Poodle descended the broken wooden steps William noticed a crouched figure at the shop window, squinting cautiously through the wheel-spokes of the Edwardian milk float. A moment later Pringle entered the shop.

'Very very quickly. Have you got anything remotely resembling some old Life Guards gear? I've been up and down Carnaby Street twice over and I'm going frantic.'

'I don't often get that kind of thing,' said William, peering wistfully at his collection of iron pineapples as if hoping he might pass them off as Guards-issue hand grenades. 'You're doing a feature on the craze for old uniforms, are you?'

'Jesus Christ, that subject's been dead for two years. The *Observer*'s done it five times, to name but one. And so have the *Sunday Times* and *Life*, but they can all go and stuff themselves because if this thing clicks I'm packing in the photography bit altogether. *Voices,* I'm talking about.'

'Voices?'

'*Lost,* as was. New title. It's called *Voices, Voices.* The point is we've got this scene where the old lady – incidentally she's not blind any more, we're going to play the whole thing straight – is rummaging through this old trunk and digs out her husband's old uniform. The link-with-the-past guff. And I've got to find the gear today because we open in Edinburgh in a couple of weeks and you' – Pringle paused dramatically – 'are going to coin a fortune.'

William raised a cautionary hand. 'My wife's downstairs and I haven't told her I'm putting money into strange theatrical ventures.'

'Yes, I know. Or at least I saw someone going downstairs and assumed it was your wife. Very rapidly, then – we're going to need the overcall.'

'I'm afraid these backstage expressions are rather beyond me.'

'When you get the contract for your investment you'll see there's a thing called the overcall. Quite simply it means that as a backer you can be called upon to put up another fifty per cent over and above what you've invested already.'

'Another hundred and twenty-five pounds?'

'More than that, I'm sorry to say. You'll recall that though you only put up two-fifty in cash, I did throw in on your behalf the one-two-five I owed you. That gives you a share of £375, so your liability is fifty per cent of that.'

'A hundred and –' William did a quick, alarming mental calculation 'eighty-seven pounds ten! But why?'

'Frankly we could do with you putting up another five hundred, but legally you only have to put a hundred and eighty-seven-ten if you want to stay in the game. *A*, the play has three sets, that costs money. *B*, we were hoping to go straight from Edinburgh to Leeds but we can't. That means we've got to keep the cast on full pay for two weeks while we try to find another date. And speaking of dates reminds me, I've got a message for you.'

'Yes?'

'She's been pestering me night and day for the last week, wanting me to get hold of you.'

Either Jackie or Rosemary. William's heart pumped into overdrive. He had no history of urgent messages from women but some masculine Ur-instinct told him to expect trouble.

'Who?'

But at this stage Poodle emerged from the basement carrying a small stone bust with part of the nose missing.

'You won't be able to sell this, will you?' She flushed slightly as she saw Pringle and observed that with a quick leap he had stationed himself by the door.

'You've met Pringle, haven't you? My wife, Poodle.'

'We have met,' said Pringle laconically.

'You're the photographer, aren't you?' said Poodle over-casually, a slight breathlessness in her voice.

'That's right,' said Pringle, toying with the door handle; and to William: 'You won't forget about that thing?'

'What was this message you had for me?' asked William hastily.

Poodle broke in: 'I was wondering if we dare ask Mr Pringle to take some pictures of Melisande. We haven't had any done for –'

'He only does magazine work. He's not a photographer in that sense, Poodle.'

'It's this bloke Jack,' said Pringle guardedly.

'Who?'

'Jack. Jack Douglas. The fellow you met down at Kemble's Club. The one with the big mouth – are you with me? An actor we know,' he added for Poodle's benefit.

'I know you only do Press work, Mr Pringle, but I thought if you'd like to come over for a drink one day . . .'

'What about *him*?' asked William, taking his tactful cue from Pringle.

'He wants you to ring him, at this number.' Pringle handed over a scrap of paper. 'He says it's urgent.'

'Say this evening, if you're not busy,' said Poodle.

'*He* didn't say what it was about?'

'Just for you to ring him.'

'Say about six? Would that be all right, William, if Mr Pringle came about six?'

'I'm a bit tied up this evening,' said Pringle with a fair display of regret. Turning back to William: 'And you won't forget that other thing?'

'What other thing?'

'Or Wednesday?' said Poodle.

'The thing. You know. The bit of paper with the figures on. The overcall. Could you put it in the post?'

'Oh.' And to change the subject William said to Poodle: 'I thought Melisande went to dancing class on Wednesday?'

'Not every week.'

'Wednesday's completely out,' said Pringle. 'I'll tell you what I'll do. Why don't we leave it over and I'll check with William and come over some other time.'

'What was all that mystery about?' asked Poodle when Pringle had left.

'I'm not quite sure,' said William honestly.

32

'Yes? It's William.'

'Oh, hello, darling. Thank you for ringing – did Pringle give you my message? I had your home number from the book but I didn't think it'd be a good idea to call you there and I couldn't find your shop number and then I ran into Pringle and he didn't have it or said he didn't have it, you know what he's like . . .'

'He tells me you want to talk to me about something,' said William tensely.

'What did he say?'

'Nothing except that it was urgent.'

'That's Pringle all over. I just asked him if he came across you to get you to call me. I was only wondering what you were up to, darling. You know? You were going to take me to dinner again, remember? and then the weeks rolled by and you didn't call – I thought you might be ill.'

William exhaled luxuriously, only realizing as he did so that he had been holding his breath from the moment of beginning to dial Jackie's number. As a by-product of his great sense of delivery he felt a limited compassion for the chattering nuisance on the other end of the telephone.

'I'm terribly sorry about not ringing you, Jackie. The fact is I've been very busy and then I lost your number and didn't know how to contact you. But I have been meaning to ask you out to dinner again for weeks.'

'That'd be lovely. You couldn't manage tonight, could you?'

'Tonight's impossible,' said William frankly.

'Or tomorrow?'

'Tomorrow's rather difficult too. I'll tell you what,' – he took a lesson from Pringle's evasive tactics in the Bucket Shop – 'now that I've got your number again, why don't 'we leave it over for the moment and –'

'Only thing is, I've got to see you as soon as possible.' Jackie's voice had risen only by perhaps an eighth. William did not know how or why he was immediately able to recognize the slight note of hysteria, and all that was behind it, since he had never been in this situation before. He made a valiant effort to integrate the development into his personality in one mighty, cynical leap – worse things happen at sea, can't make omelettes without breaking eggs – but he was left only with a sensation of constant hot water in his stomach.

'Why?' he said pointlessly, his own voice higher. 'Is there something wrong?'

'Well, yes, darling, there bloody well is. But there are people coming in and out and Mrs Wallace will be back any minute so I don't really want to say anything on the telephone.'

'Can't you give me some idea?' (He clutched pathetically at his last straw. If only he were a man with pub acquaintances he might yet have an anecdote to tell: 'I was sweating on the top line. I'd never been so scared in all my life.')

Jackie said: 'Just imagine the worst possible thing that could have happened, that's all.'

'Oh, Christ,' said William. It was useless, he supposed, to hope that Jackie had taken on some of the characteristics of Rosemary, who would have started the conversation claiming to be four months' pregnant and finished up admitting that she was mildly worried about being two days overdue.

'But you're not to worry,' said Jackie. 'Everything's organized. I know this man who's a friend of a friend and he's very discreet and very reliable and very safe. Only I do have to see you. So can we meet for a drink at say seven?'

'Seven. That's something of an awkward time.'

'You do know what I'm talking about, love, don't you?'

'I think so.'

'Then don't you think you'd better make a bit of an effort and be there?'

'Yes. I suppose I ought.'

33

But Pringle, I *don't* want to bother you, I just want to know why you're avoiding me.'

'I'm not avoiding you, ducky, but I don't know why you have to keep ringing me up every three minutes.'

'I've rung you four times this week, that's all, and half a dozen times before that at most, and this is the first time you've ever answered.'

'Because I know who's ringing, my flower. I daren't pick up the bloody receiver. I daren't even go out of the house in case you're hanging about outside.'

'Well you started it. I was a perfectly happily married woman before you came along. You can't just pick somebody up and put them down like that.'

'What did you expect me to do?'

'Exactly that, I suppose.'

'Well, then.'

'It's no use saying "Well, then."'

'What do you want me to say?'

'Something. You could be more encouraging. Why were you so horrible to me in the Bucket Shop?'

'I couldn't be anything else but, my flower. What would Weary William have said if I'd given you a quick grope?'

'There are other places. I tried to get you to come back home with me but you wouldn't cotton on.'

'Not my style, baby.'

'Can I ask you one question, then? Are you ever going to see me again?'

'Well, I'm not a great one for the big dramatic scenes.'

'Why do you say dramatic scenes? There won't *be* any dramatic ... I won't be any trouble. I wasn't any trouble before, was I? I mean, it's not as if I'd be hanging round your neck.'

'Well, let's leave it like this. I'm going away for a bit. I'll get in touch with you when I come back.'

'You won't, though, will you?'

34

The drink with Jackie was not the ordeal he feared it was going to be. She explained her position calmly and, for her, lucidly. Scrupulously, though not with malice, she sealed off all the remaining avenues of hope. Yes, she was sure. Yes, she had seen her doctor. Yes, it had been confirmed. She was six weeks pregnant. She had no idea how it had happened. They had both had a bit to drink that night and she supposed she hadn't been as careful as she ought to have been. She was sorry.

'You said something about knowing somebody,' said William. He wanted to get to this point quickly for he was terrified in case she began to talk about adoption or, even worse, raising the child herself. He had conjured up a hideous vision of an elaborate double life wherein he shuttled backwards and forwards between Tulip Street and Jackie's basement flat, smuggling rag books under his jacket, flitting the child through Regents Park on quick, secretive walks, and cutting corners off Poodle's housekeeping money to pay for its education.

'There's this friend of a friend,' said Jackie again. 'He's very Harley Street but of course he's very costly. It's fantastic what these people charge but they get away with it and it's all tax-free.' She then sought to divert William with a long story of a famous surgeon who was supposed to have paid for his country house with money produced from a suitcase in bundles of a thousand.

'I must say you're being very cheerful about all this,' said William.

'There's no point in being down-in-mouth, is there? And it's not the end of the world, darling, in this day and age.'

She was so self-possessed that he couldn't help wondering if she hadn't been in this situation before. He bet himself, rather sourly, that she had, but at the same time he was grateful to be in experienced hands.

He was beginning to feel a little better. Jackie had gone into a side-anecdote about the incompetence of her mother's doctor, and the rotating lips were having something of their usual soporific effect. From feeling sick and frightened he was now cautiously experimenting with the blasé outlook he had attempted earlier: the man of the world who has had his fun and must pay for it. He did not know quite how to phrase the question that now had priority in his mind. 'How much?' seemed a little too blunt. 'What do you think it might cost?' would sound as if he were going to haggle over his responsibilities.

But Jackie, who might have been divining his thoughts, suddenly brought her digression to an end with:

'. . . and then he has the nerve to charge her three guineas a visit. My Harley Street man might cost the earth but at least he'll do what he's paid to do. Only it's two hundred pounds, darling, and I know it's all a bit "B" picture but he wants it in fivers.'

'Two hundred. H'm.' He rubbed his chin like a bargain-hunter in the Bucket Shop, as if expecting that with a measure of hesitation on his part Jackie might offer a large discount.

'I'm afraid so. Can you manage it?'

'I shall have to, won't I?'

On reflection he thought this retort might sound ungracious, so he took her hand and squeezed it. Jackie responded by puckering her great mouth and making a loud kissing noise.

'It could be worse, darling. At least I know where to go and we're not running round in frantic circles trying to find somebody.'

– a fact of which William was only too conscious. There had been another question hovering in his mind, and this too he had difficulty in phrasing. 'How do I know it's me?'/'Are you sure I'm the only one concerned?'/'Couldn't it possibly have been someone else?' In grateful acknowledgement of Jackie's expert management of the affair, he decided to leave the question open.

35

Poodle had not been picked up for a long time and scarcely knew how to go about it. She thought seriously about making a train journey to St Albans and back, having heard during her girlhood there of women being molested in railway carriages. But she did not want to be saddled with a lover who would expect her to travel thirty miles to his home or, if he were married, who would meet her at King's Cross station and hold her hand in sooty public houses. She would have liked to have gone on a cruise, but that was not possible.

She knew, because she and William sometimes used to drop in for a drink and a crab sandwich in the days when they still went occasionally to the theatre, that there were several cocktail lounges in the St James's area. There was one that had a quilted bar and angular fluted mirrors belonging to the nineteen-thirties – a survival, she supposed, of the days when 'men-about-town' had rooms in Jermyn Street and chose their mistresses from the musical comedy of the moment. The kind of man who used it nowadays gave it the ambience of a temporary officers' mess or perhaps the salesmen's private bar at the Motor Show; but she could remember that at the little round glass tables there sometimes sat unaccompanied women, nibbling olives – and she seemed to remember that they were never unaccompanied for long.

She was not quite sure what she was looking for. Nobody single, for the kind of single men who used these places, all ginger moustaches, panatellas and gin and tonics, were stamped 'bachelor' in the sense of it being an old-fashioned trade mark like Monkey Brand or Gentlemen's Relish. She imagined them living in small tidy flats with an electric plate on which they heated ready-made curries. Their dearest possessions would be a pair of ivory-backed hairbrushes and they would turn out either to be impotent or to have unpleasant sexual habits. But there were other men, more portly, more respectable, who carried briefcases and dashed off for eight o'clock trains. How reluctantly did they knock back the last whisky before going home to their lady wives? Or did they always go home? Did they sometimes walk slowly through Soho, catching the strip-club photographs with a practised eye-corner? When they pined for a sexual renaissance in their ordered lives, did they ever think that their dreams might be easily and discreetly fulfilled?

Poodle had several grave doubts about her mission. It was one thing to get herself picked up, another to disengage herself should her sponsor not prove suitable. She would want guarantees that he would not interfere with her private life nor expect her to involve herself in his, that he would be available (within reason) on demand, that he would be able to provide suitable premises, and that he should be ready, in fact eager, for an entirely functional relationship.

Poodle wondered about gigolos, who seemed to be out of fashion. Then she had another idea. She went and sought the counsel of the homosexual brothers who owned Trousers Primarily.

'How much is that cravat thing?'

'Fifteen bob, dear. Give us a big sloppy kiss and you can have it for ten.'

'Do you think William would like it?'

'Not unless he's on the turn,' said the second brother. This brought Poodle within striking distance of her theme.

'Will you both tell me something, if I ask you?'

The first brother made a pretence of bridling and said: 'If you want to know who does what and to whom, the answer is that he does the cooking and I do the washing-up.'

'No, seriously! Is it true that people who are – well, you know . . .'

'She's going to say it, she's going to *say* it!' the first brother screeched, clapping his hands.

'All right, then, *queer*,' said Poodle, going a rich red. 'I wish I hadn't started this now, but is it true that a lot of them, you know, have the best of both worlds?'

The brothers, who were not used to direct questioning of this kind, were somewhat put out. The second one tried to look baffled. The first one took refuge in a series of little petting sounds, and explained:

'She means AC-DC. Don't you, poppet?'

'Yes.'

'Ambisextrous.'

'Yes.'

'Two for the price of one.'

'*Yes.*'

The first brother sought hard for more synonyms. The second brother, who was beginning to look belligerent, put in:

'What about it?'

'Well, is it *true*?'

'Is what true?'

Poodle drew a deep breath.

'That people who are AC-DC or ambi-whatever are only too pleased to hop into bed with the nearest available girl?'

The second brother stared at her. The first one, noticeably embarrassed, made a great show of flapping his wrists and

began to say 'OOoh!' and 'My *dear!*' and 'You little sauce-
box!' until he had disappeared completely behind the visor of
self-caricature.

She settled for the cocktail bars of St James's,

36

The worst part so far had been getting two hundred pounds in
fivers out of the bank without creating the impression of a
fool and his money about to be parted. 'To do some business
in the East End junk markets – these people always prefer
ready cash,' was the explanation he had ready, but the cashier
was not very interested.

William had sealed the money in an envelope and was now
much exercised about how to hand it to Jackie without awk-
wardness. He had arranged to meet her for lunch to conclude
the transaction. He agreed with himself that since it was to all
intents and purposes a business lunch the proper course would
be to conduct a light conversation during the food and give
her the money over coffee. Accordingly, when Jackie opened
her handbag for a cigarette at the end of the meal, he dropped
the envelope into it. She smiled her acknowledgement and continued with her synopsis of a television play in which she might
have been playing the second lead but for the producer's mistaken belief that she could not do a Liverpool accent. The
matter of her abortion, which was to be carried out the next
evening, was not referred to.

37

From the *Encyclopaedia Britannica* he learned that the over-
all mortality rate of legitimate therapeutic abortion was about
one per cent, but that the undiscoverable death rate of
criminal abortion was reckoned to be relatively higher.
Jackie's arrangements with her Harley Street friend of a friend
seemed to fall between these two definitions. William gave her

odds of fifty to one and resigned himself to a couple of sleepless nights.

He had only begun to occupy himself with this aspect after handing over the money. He went straight from the restaurant to Fulham Reference Library. The *Encyclopaedia* was very firm on one point: that not only the person who caused an abortion but anyone who contributed to the act (anyone who paid for it, he surmised, was liable to conviction of crime, unless the health, life or reason of the mother were clearly jeopardized.

'Daddy, what's prison like?' asked Melisande that evening, as he sat gazing sightlessly at *A Man of Property*.

William, who had been musing on Jackie's health and reason, was startled.

'Why on earth do you ask that?'

'We were learning about that king today.'

'What king?'

'That king in prison.'

'Yes, but *which* king in prison? Edward the Second, Henry the – Sixth, was it? Or who?'

'I think he was a bad king.'

'Which bad king?'

'I don't know, daddy.'

'Don't be ridiculous. If you'd pay some attention to your lessons instead of ...' But Melisande's face began to crumple and she was suppressing a sniffle. Poodle was out somewhere and Lil the baby-sitter had gone home; William did not want to cope with a tantrum on his own. In any case his own knowledge of history was too sketchy for him to pursue his point. 'All right, then, get on with it.'

'Miss Holland said his bed was a bundle of straw and his only friend was a mouse,' said Melisande, visibly agitated.

William softened at this hint of sensitivity in his daughter.

'Yes, but it's not like that nowadays. Prisons are very enlightened places. Do you know what enlightened means?'

'They have lots of windows.'

'Well, something like that. The prisoners are allowed to read books and play games and watch television. And some places don't even have bars – they're more or less like farms, and the prisoners work in the fields and sleep in big dormitories.' William had hopefully cast for himself a billet in Ford Open Prison. He saw the doctor who actually performed the operation getting two years, and himself twelve months.

'Do they put children in prison, daddy?'

'Good heavens, no.'

And then, to his surprise and horror, Melisande began to cry. Her lower lip quivered, her forehead throbbed and she threw herself into his arms, the tears running across her face into her ear.

'There! It's all right! Of course they don't put children in prison.'

'The l-l-lady in the swee-hee-heetshop said they do!'

'Then she's a very stupid lady. Why should she want to say a thing like that?'

'I don't – hoop – know.'

'But surely she didn't just say it out of the blue? Why did she tell you they put children in prison?'

'I don't *hoop*!'

'Are you sure you don't know?'

'Hoop.'

'Well, I think you do.'

Melisande raised a blotchy face from his jacket.

'You'll tell hoop! hoop!'

'I'll tell mummy what?'

'What the – hoop – lady in the swee-hee-hee-hee . . .'

'That'll do, Melisande! Tell me what the lady in the sweetshop said and I promise I won't tell mummy.' He reached for a Kleenex and wiped her streaming nose. Melisande, between spasms of weeping, was darting out her tongue and licking the area above her upper lip in a manner which he found distasteful. 'Now just calm down and tell me all about it.'

'I was just ho-ho-holding a box of hoop – hoop – hoop!'

'A box of what?'

'A box of cho-hoh-hoh-hoh . . .'

'All right, you were holding a box of chocolates. Why were you holding a box of chocolates?'

'I'd just bought a Mars bar-har-har and I was going out of the hoop and I picked up a box of hoop-hoop-hoop and was loo-hoo-*hooking* at them.'

'You were looking at a box of chocolates. And then what happened?'

'The lady said – hoop – hoop!'

'Calmly, now.'

'Hoop! Hoop!'

'Come along.'

'She said I'd hoop – hoop – hoop – hoop!'

'Melisande! At once!'

'She said I'd taken them and that little girls like me went to prison and that if I went into the sho-hoh-hop again she'd fetch a polee-hee-hee-hee-heecema-a-a-n!'

'It's all right, Melisande. It's all right. It's all right.'

38

'What it boils down to, then, is that we've lost all our money?'

'We did get marvellous reviews in Edinburgh,' said Pringle. 'But as bad luck would have it we clashed with *Hello, Dolly* at the Lyceum. The audiences weren't paying to come in, we were a thousand over budget – which I've still got to find, if you've got any ideas – and we just didn't have the loot to keep the play going. Pity.'

'And I lose everything I've put in – two-fifty plus a hundred and eighty-seven pounds ten – four hundred and thirty-odd pounds?'

'You're not the only one. What about Desmond Higgins, the poor bloody author? He hocked his house and furniture and he's three thousand up the spout. And I personally am down two-fifty, which I had to borrow.'

'You do remember that you still have an outstanding bill with me for a hundred and twenty-five?'

'You've had that, my old sport. It was part of the deal, if you remember.'

'So in round figures I can say good-bye to well over five hundred pounds, and I shan't see a penny of it back?'

'Not a sausage,' said Pringle cheerfully.

This interlude served, for half an hour, to take William's mind off Jackie. Her operation, if all had gone smoothly, would have taken place the previous evening. There was nothing in the papers about the arrest of a doctor or a girl's body being found in strange circumstances in a back room in Harley Street. But William by no means considered himself to be out of the wood yet. He had been doing some supplementary reading about medical complications and he had spent a good part of his day brooding over tetanus and its effects.

He had made no arrangements with Jackie about the transmission of news of her safe delivery. He wished now that he had asked her to send a cryptic telegram: GOODS DESPATCHED OK (or possibly something phrased a little more delicately). He had, however, taken the precaution of telling Poodle that he had a meeting with some furniture people and would be home late, for he intended at six o'clock to take a cab to Jackie's basement flat in Marylebone Lane and reassure himself that she was in good health again. He was not happy about this decision, for he could see her going straight from the nursing home to visit her mother or one of her numerous friends in the gown trade, and he would be left standing under a lamp-post through the long cold hours of evening, with sweat on his forehead.

But when he locked up the Bucket Shop and went out into the Fulham Road, Jackie was waiting for him in a doorway opposite. He thought at first that she had come to give him the terrible news that her Harley Street friend of a friend had found her condition too dangerous to risk an operation, but as he crossed to meet her he saw her wide, wet smile and knew that her ordeal, and his, was over.

'I didn't like to come into the shop in case your family was around.' She always referred to his wife obliquely as 'your family'; not for the first time William felt a quick pulse of gratitude for the broad strokes of euphemism which in Jackie passed for tact. 'I just thought you'd like to know I've survived and that everything's all right.'

Again he was touched.

'I was going to come and see you this evening, just to make sure.'

'I thought you might but I'm just popping round to see my mother and I didn't want you to find me out and start worrying. Oh, and I've brought you this, love.'

She fished from her handbag the same envelope that he had given her in the restaurant two days earlier. It had been ripped open, and contained ten five-pound notes.

'It seems I was overcharging you. He only wanted one-fifty. So now you can afford to buy us both an extremely large drink.'

The process of love was something totally foreign to William: he had never encountered it and would not have recognized it. But he had known several moments of tenderness in his life – they were few, and he had them tabulated. Three of them were to do with Jackie. Once, when she had told him after sleeping with him that he was not to regard himself as being committed to her in any way. The second, when she had just now taken the trouble to come and tell him that all was well. And now, when she had voluntarily refunded his fifty pounds. Jackie was not well-off or even solvent; she was perpetually unemployed in her vocation and she had to work in a wretched cake shop to pay her rent. William could not think of anyone – Rosemary or Poodle or anyone else – who in her circumstances would not have quietly pocketed the money. He felt a sudden, fierce regard for her lasting all the way through their first vodka and tonic, when there began to seem a danger that she might implicate him in a quiet dinner somewhere. Some of the pub's homely patrons were staring at his flamboyant companion, and he began to worry about Tulip Street being only around the corner, and about how to extricate himself.

39

The barman crossed from table to table with bowls of crisps. When his tray was empty he approached Poodle.

'Is there anything I can do for you, madam?'

'You could let me have some more of those olives, thank you.'

'I was wondering if you was like waiting for somebody. Whether you wanted to telephone.'

'Surely I'm entitled to sit here with a drink?'

'Certainly, madam. Sit here as long as you please. Only strictly speaking, we're not supposed to serve unescorted ladies.'

The barman, unblinking, seemed unaware of contradicting himself. Poodle could not decide whether this stare was solicitous or impertinent. It was probable that he was just bored. The bar had plainly become unfashionable and in four visits Poodle had counted a total of only five customers, none of whom had taken any notice of her.

'You'd better let me have my bill.'

'Eighteen shillings, madam. It's company policy, see. Whereas you could come in on the odd occasion, strictly speaking I'm not allowed to let you make a habit of it.'

'I think I want two shillings change,' said Poodle.

40

William had never known her so quarrelsome as when she got home this evening, and he hesitated a long time before telling her that their projected holiday in Ireland would have to be cancelled. Besides the deprivations of Pringle and Jackie his deposit account had suffered a demand from the Inland Revenue and – what in fatter times would have come out of the profits of the Bucket Shop – this month's mortgage repayment on the house. He had less than two hundred pounds in the bank.

He approached the subject by a roundabout route.

'You didn't tell me you were going to be out this evening?'

'I've been round to Mary Fitzgibbon's. Do you object?' This was a friend of Poodle's flat-sharing days who was now safely in Africa somewhere with an engineer. William had never questioned the revival of the friendship nor asked Poodle to invite Mary Fitzgibbon to dinner.

'I just thought if you'd let me know when you're going to

be out I could arrange to come home early and you wouldn't have to pay the baby-sitter.'

'I only give her five bob. Does it make all that much difference?'

'I happen to be going through a pretty lean period at the shop just at present and all these five bobs count.'

'If we had an au pair girl like everyone else you wouldn't have to pay for a baby-sitter.'

Privately William agreed with this oft-mooted argument. He saw a succession of foreign girls passing through the house – some French and scatterbrained, who would provide material for comic anecdotes; some Scandinavian and beautiful, who would fall in love with him; others Germanic, dumpy and stupid who would hang the mattresses out of the window and bring colour to Tulip Street.

But this was not the point.

'When we can afford an au pair girl we'll have one. Meanwhile I don't think Melisande ought to be left with a baby-sitter not much older than herself. Lil's not a good influence for one thing and for another Melisande's at a stage when we ought to be spending more time with her.'

'By "we" I suppose you mean me?'

'I mean both of us or either of us. She's going through a very awkward phase at the moment.'

'What awkward phase? What are you talking about?'

The truth was that William did not know. Although much given to self-analysis he shrank from investigating the psyches of other people, including his daughter. He was in general terms perturbed about Melisande, and when he had some free time he would have to go a bit more deeply into the significance of her traumatic experience at the sweetshop. Meanwhile he felt that by voicing his concern to Poodle he had discharged his responsibility for the moment and he was now anxious to reach his main problem, get that disposed of, and settle down with a book.

'I feel Melisande might sometimes be conscious of an atmosphere of strain at home. You're often short-tempered with her and so am I. I don't blame either of us for this – it's been a trying year and ordinarily I'd say we both need a holiday.

But things have been very quiet at the shop lately and I'm afraid it's going to be a case of cutting our cloth according to our ...' Aware of having misquoted the proverb, he tailed off.

'What's that supposed to mean?' asked Poodle.

'That we shan't be able to go to Ireland after all.'

'You don't seriously mean that?'

'I'm afraid so.'

'You do know that the only break I get from one year's end to another, the only time I'm able to forget about this bloody house and this bloody street, is when we go on holiday?'

'I'm sorry, but there it is.'

'"I'm sorry, but there it is!"' jeered Poodle. 'You are a bastard William, aren't you?'

Delighted at having reached his point so cleverly, he had not really prepared himself for a reaction, certainly not one so savage. He pulled himself out of a reverie of self-congratulations to say guardedly:

'I don't see why.'

'*You think I don't know, don't you?*'

– That you gave Pringle £437 to invest in a ludicrous flop, that you paid for an abortion: these accusations signalled themselves to William at priority rates. Hastily re-manning his defences, he was preparing some emergency propaganda on the dangers of listening to ill-founded gossip when to his great relief Poodle proved to have got hold of the wrong end of the stick.

'I'm *perfectly* aware what you've done with your money, William. You've been filling that shop for months and months with useless rubbish. You drew out two hundred and fifty pounds not long ago, then a hundred and eighty-seven pounds ten, then two hundred pounds only the other day. And please don't deny it because your bank statement came today and I looked at it.'

'If you must look at my bank statement then you'll know the straits we're in without my –'

'What straits? What are you talking about, "straits"? Why are you always coming out with these stupid words? "Straits!" You've spent all that money on junk with no idea about how or when or if you're ever going to see it again and then you calmly turn around and –'

'I have not spent it on junk, I have invested it in stock,' said William coldly. Not only did he readily adapt himself to Poodle's interpretation of his extravagance: such was his chameleon nature that he felt genuinely hurt at what, accepting that she had got her facts right, he could only see as an unjust accusation. 'If you took any interest in my business at all you'd know that there is a time to buy and a time to sell –'

'And the time to buy is just when we're looking forward to a holiday?'

'In this case, yes. Just to give you one example. Goss china at present is going dirt cheap – there's too much of it on the market. In three or four months, when winter's approaching and people are wondering how they can cheer up their homes a little, it will begin to fetch high prices.'

William had read this in a trade magazine, although about brass candlesticks and not Goss china, of which he had possessed three full teachests since first opening the Bucket Shop. His still genuine indignation was now polluted by small traces of self-disgust at catching himself pretending to know more about his profession than he did. He continued, however (Poodle had lit a cigarette and was walking abstractedly about the room like an actress learning a part) to produce further examples, adapted from what he had read; soon he had reassured himself, if not her, that he was a shrewd businessman with a breathless flair for the calculated risk.

When he had finished Poodle began quietly to deliver the lines she had rehearsed.

'Well, you'll go bankrupt eventually, won't you?'

'I hardly think so,' said William uneasily, for the suggestion made him nervous. He wondered if Poodle were right and he had in fact been over-buying. He had forgotten by now that the whole argument was based on a fiction.

'You're in a business you know nothing about, William. You've no talent for it, I don't think you even have a real interest in it. I'd tell you to close the Bucket Shop and get a job but what could you do? What are you good for?'

'I can do anything I've a mind to,' retorted William.

'Possibly I could do a little better if I had some help and encouragement from my wife.'

'Why?'

'Well, isn't it usual?'

Poodle had not had the best of evenings. It was not that she had been unable to get herself picked up: she had come to enjoy her solitary dry Martini, followed by a stroll past the expensive shops of St James's before catching the bus home. Even the barman's rudeness had not unduly put her out: there were other bars, and other barmen. But pausing in Jermyn Street to look in a perfumier's window she had been approached by a police constable who, assuming her to be a prostitute, advised her to get on out of it. When Poodle protested the constable, instead of apologizing for his error, quoted the Metropolitan Police (Powers) Act and threatened to arrest her for loitering. She had arrived home in a mood of angry self-pity, convinced that the world was in conspiracy to rob her of her small pleasures.

'William, I don't know why you should expect help or encouragement, or sympathy, or anything else from me. You never give me anything. You spend your entire time when you're at home snapping at Melisande or prowling about straightening newspapers. You criticize all the time and I wouldn't mind if you had something to criticize.'

'A good deal, in this house.'

'Small things. Niggardly things.'

'Or detail, if one cared to put it that way. I have an eye for detail and I prefer the details to be right.'

'As for example when Melisande's worrying about her homework and the only contribution you can make is to nag her to sit up straight or go on about her using double negatives.'

'It'll do her no harm to learn how to speak properly or how to sit properly. And I do help her with her homework, which is more than can be said for you.'

'Yes, well the house doesn't run itself.'

'I thought it did, largely.'

The argument, to Poodle's disgust, began to close in on the familiar round of domestic grievances. She felt seriously frustrated, like someone who has been interrupted in coition. She had been hoping for a proper discussion of her marriage; it was not often that she had the case against William marshalled properly in her mind and she could have held the floor without difficulty for some time, cataloguing his shortcomings and the defects in his character, charting the slow deterioration of the marriage from its indifferent beginnings.

She tried once to restore the discussion to a broader basis:

'When you talk about my failure, William, you're really talking about your own.'

'We'll discuss my failure when you've explained in one sentence why it's necessary to leave spent matches on every window-sill when we have at least two dozen ashtrays.'

Poodle was going to add: 'Do you know for example how rotten you are in bed?' but instead she walked out of the room.

William sat in front of the electric radiator, his mouth working as he continued the argument in his imagination. Poodle paced the bedroom.

Both fumed independently for half an hour.

Then Poodle, wearing her dressing gown and smoking her tenth cigarette of the evening, re-appeared.

'If you don't want or can't afford to go to Ireland, William, that's your own business. But I thought I'd better make it clear that Melisande and I are going to have a holiday this year, come what may.'

'Oh? What on?'

I don't know and I don't care. If I can only take her down to Brighton she's going to have a holiday.'

'It doesn't concern you at all what problems I might have in finding the money?'

'I don't want to hear about your problems, William.'

He rose stiffly.

'Then I'm going out.'

'Bloody go out,' said Poodle.

41

He was becoming an expert on unhappiness and its various constituents. He was familiar so far with the unhappiness of frustration, of anxiety, of jealousy, envy, fear, insecurity, lethargy, inadequacy, uncertainty, embarrassment, unfulfilment, anger, disappointment, guilt, hypochondria, temporary impotence and limited physical pain (he was rarely more depressed than when conscious that the only thing he had to be concerned about was an ulcer on his tongue or that he had cut his nostril while shaving). He did not believe in spiritual or general unhappiness. It was his practice when in low spirits to analyse his mood and separate its elements; he could thus readily detect the superficial effects of ennui, central heating or the symptoms of flu and isolate the more concrete sources of his unrest. He would then decide what steps he could take to remove or avoid the irritating factor, in the belief that he would then achieve peace of mind.

Having slammed out of the house he walked furiously along Tulip Street reviewing his argument with Poodle so that he might locate the portion or portions of it which had disturbed him most. He was well into the Fulham Road before he realized that his thoughtstream was running completely cross-current to his mood, and that far from being unhappy he was filled with a great sense of liberation.

'Bloody go out,' Poodle had said, with no interest in where he was going or what time he might return. This was virtually the first time in his married life, certainly the first time so late at night, when he had found himself a free agent without having first to chisel out an elaborate, top-heavy excuse and then, in a voice grown breathless with the effort of sounding casual and convincing, produce it for Poodle's scrutiny.

She had spoken, too, of taking Melisande away on holiday with her and leaving him to his own devices. He put aside his financial problems: if Poodle went away it would be the first time for over nine years that they had not shared the same bed.

Contemplating these bonuses, William was able to trace the main source of his elation. He had never questioned that he was answerable to Poodle for his movements, and she to him. There was a contract between them and any breach of it was answerable by heavy penalties of guilt, deceit and worry. But in Poodle's demonstration against him tonight there had been, if one looked for them, intimations of a new régime, a loosening of the bonds. Reviewing their argument in this interesting new light William saw it as an important landmark: a declaration that they had abandoned the convention whereby their lives were irrevocably bound together and that henceforth what touched one did not necessarily touch them both. They would never go back – they might indeed go forward. Theirs might become a union of independent partners, like the adult marriages one read about in enlightened magazines.

He drank in the night air and worked his shoulders like a man who has been relieved of a heavy load. He began to budget for Poodle's holiday with Melisande, but the figures could not lodge in his mind for the vision that was forming there of sunny breakfasts in the Kenco Coffee House, small dinners in Soho and night after squandered night of freedom.

It was only eleven o'clock. He looked for a taxi.

42

A psychiatrist had once described Jackie as a potential manic-depressive. Her constant flow of words, he said, masked a basic insecurity; her great aptitude for being snubbed indicated a strong desire for self-destruction. This was not in a consulting room but at a party, and the psychiatrist was so drunk that he could not pronounce the word 'masochist'. Jackie, however, was deeply impressed by his perception. Before falling down the stairs he gave her his home telephone number, his consulting room number, and the numbers of two hospitals and a child guidance clinic where he sometimes advised, begging her to ring him the next day. She did so, at all the numbers, several times, but he no longer wanted to speak to her. This was the pattern of Jackie's life.

The gown manufacturers who were her friends made no pretence that she was anything but a convenience. They called her when they were in town for a couple of days from Leeds or Manchester, and sometimes they would press her to receive colleagues of theirs and be nice to them. In this way, Jackie widened her circle of acquaintances. She never turned down an invitation, and if at the end of an evening someone slipped a five-pound note into her hand she did not refuse it, although she was careful never to solicit gifts of money.

Her other friends were the actors who gathered in Kemble's Club. They were often rude to her, or ignored her altogether; but sometimes, very late at night, one of them who was drunk would warm towards her and eventually take her home. Thereafter, she had noticed, he would avoid her, even to the point of leaving the club hurriedly when she entered it. She put this down to a fear of getting involved.

Some of Kemble's members regarded her as a bore: she knew this because they had told her so. Jackie would concede that she talked about herself a great deal; before the drunken psychiatrist analysed the tendency as basic insecurity she had always thought that she was demonstrating her unquenchable optimism – 'keeping my pecker up' was what she called it. She did get very depressed sometimes. She thought a lot and talked a lot about her seven months in New York in the high camp production of *The Student Prince*. She had seemed then to be at the beginning of a career; American businessmen had taken her out and bought her whisky sours, and even the English theatre colony had tolerated her at their parties as a working actress.

She had not worked for a long time. She had the impression that the gown manufacturers called her less often than they used to – her gas bill was higher, and she was using more coffee. Sometimes she could not pretend that the members of Kemble's Club turned their shoulders on her only because they were talking business. She was very glad about William. She took his silence for sympathy and his nervousness for sensitivity. She saw in him great qualities of loyalty and understanding. Diffidence was not a quality with which she was very familiar, and she categorized it as gentleness. When her door bell rang at ten minutes to twelve and William, drenched to the skin, stood on the mat, she was delighted to see him.

'I walked most of the way. I couldn't get a cab.'

'Come in and take your clothes off, darling. You'll catch double pneumonia.'

'You don't mind my turning up out of the blue at this hour?'

'Of course I don't.'

As she helped William out of his shirt she said, 'You know we won't be able to do anything tonight, don't you?'

'I just wanted to see you.'

'I hoped you did.'

43

He began to see Jackie regularly, offering Poodle only the skimpiest excuses for his absence. They went at first to various Soho restaurants, which William found economically a strain; but then they discovered a trattoria in Marylebone High Street and began to eat there. They no longer automatically went on to clubs and night clubs but formed the habit of returning early to the flat with a bottle of cheap wine. This suited William: it was easier on his pocket, he did not have the worry of wondering if he could make love with too much drink inside him, and he was able to get home before midnight.

Jackie, he found, was a good listener as well as an inexorable talker. He once told her the story of his life, with several anecdotes about his Air Force life equal in length and substance, or lack of it, to the ones she told him; he found to his surprise that she had let him talk for two hours. He never discussed his marriage, although she occasionally asked politely after his family, but he did manage to convey the impression that the flat in Marylebone Lane was a haven of peace in a troubled existence.

This was substantially true. Since their quarrel Poodle had been treating him, not as a stranger but as a casual acquaintance. On the evenings he spent at home she was either out or busy in some other region of the house. She would produce meals only if he had ordered them in advance; on the other hand, if he did come home for dinner she was prepared to sit with him at the dining table, chatting on neutral topics as if they had just met in a Pullman car.

Melisande was being difficult. Her voice had always had the makings of a whine and now with proper nurturing this early promise had been fulfilled. She exasperated him more than ever and he could not bear to talk to her for long.

The shop was doing badly.

Jackie soothed him. She never asked him questions, stopped him leaving when it was time for him to go, nor tried to cajole him into meeting her when it was difficult for him. She never insisted on going out when he wanted to stay in, nor on making love when he didn't feel up to it. She didn't expect him to be concerned in her problems or to talk about his own. She unfolded her interminable stories before him like an experienced salesman showing samples: glad if he showed an interest and asked her to elaborate a point, not offended if his eyes glazed over and he nodded and smiled politely.

He began to lose the fear which had exercised him at the beginning of their relationship of being trapped or compromised. He no longer lay awake at night imagining Jackie turning up at his house or writing him letters. When he arranged an evening with her he would even look forward to seeing her again instead of asking himself if and how he should cancel the arrangement.

Once, when Poodle had said something unusually cutting, he caught himself wondering if he might be in love with Jackie. After due thought he came out against any such imprudent emotion but concluded that she made him feel – 'wanted' was too strong a word: he would have felt suspicious and alarmed at being wanted. But she made him feel that he was important to her, and that the circumference of his existence had widened to include someone other than himself. Also, she was by and large an attractive girl. She was an actress after all, and it gratified him that she should have chosen him from the range of men obviously at her command. Sometimes while they sat in the flat drinking wine and talking, one of her gown manufacturers would ring. Before agreeing to go out with him she would always put her hand on the receiver and say: 'Are we doing anything on Thursday?' It pleased William that she was in demand, but put him first.

44

One night after he had been with Jackie, Rosemary was waiting for him at the end of Tulip Street. She had telephoned him several times since her return to London but William had always hung up on her without speaking.

'I know you don't want to see me but there's something I've got to explain to you.'

'You'll have to make it very quick, then. It's late.' Checking his own emotional pulse, William was satisfied to get a count of normal. He had no curiosity about what Rosemary was doing there, no feelings of apprehension or panic, and, more important, no sense of dread concerning what she had been up to since he saw her last.

'I've been thinking about what went wrong between us.'

'Nothing went wrong,' said William courteously. 'Everything comes to an end, and we came to an end.'

'I don't see how that can be true. You once said I was the most important person in your life.'

He remembered saying this, and a number of other things that now seemed equally ludicrous. At one time such a statement would have seemed as binding upon him as an indenture. 'Well,' he said, looking at his watch, 'you aren't now.'

'I know why you're being like this, William, and I think I hate myself as much as you do, if not more so. All this started when you guessed that I'd been to bed with Pringle, didn't it? And I stupidly denied it? And then you goaded me into telling you about those others.'

'Ah, the cricket team.'

'I know you're very bitter about it. I must have hurt you badly.'

'I shouldn't worry too much about that.'

'I can understand why you didn't want to see me and why you wouldn't talk to me on the phone. I just threw those men at you like a bunch of fireworks and left you to get over it on your own, as best you could. I didn't tell you what had happened or why it had happened or how it had happened.'

All this in the low voice, her downcast eyes measuring the shadow of the shopblind under which she and William stood. Rosemary paused to give him the chance to say something bitter, or to prompt her, so that they could begin their catechism. But he was pointedly silent.

'Shall I go on?'

'I'd just as soon that you didn't.'

'I don't want to, believe me. I'm so ashamed of myself and I just want to pretend that none of those people existed. But I didn't realize until I went away and could think more clearly that this wasn't fair on you and that I just couldn't shut off the past as though it had nothing to do with you. If it had all happened before I met you it would have been different, but it didn't, and I can see now that you were entitled to know everything that I'd done. So, if you want me to, starting with Pringle and working backwards or forwards or any way you like, I'll tell you everything you want to know.'

Rosemary had given a lot of thought to this move. Usually after William quarrelled with her his masochistic obsession with her transgressions brought him back to her within a week or a fortnight at most. This was a longer rift than normal and Rosemary could only conclude that he was building up a dangerous immunity to her treatment. A massive overdose seemed to be called for. Accordingly she had in readiness a detailed file on each of her eleven lovers, some of the data fictitious, much of it true, plus some supplementary revelations about recent adventures calculated to turn William's hair white.

She was nonplussed when he said:

'It's very kind of you but it's after midnight and I do have to be up early tomorrow.'

'You don't want me to tell you?'

'No, thank you.'

'Because it would upset you too much?'

A silence, which Rosemary misjudged. She went on:

'It *will* upset you, it's no use pretending otherwise, but probably some of the things aren't as bad as you imagine.'

William was not good on timing, but for once he was sure that he had got his cue exactly right. At what he was about to say he felt an almost spiritual sense of joy. He spoke carefully, cobbling his reply together from phrases he had picked up from Pringle.

'Rosemary, I don't care if you've been buggered twelve times by twenty-five negroes, one after the other, in public, hanging by your heels from a chandelier. I don't want to know because *I'm not interested*.'

Rosemary stared at him. William looked back benignly.

She comprehended.

'You've been out with somebody else tonight, haven't you?'

'Yes.'

'Can I ask who?'

'Nobody you'd know. An actress,' said William offhandedly.

Rosemary lowered her thick eyelids. Her face set in the familiar sullen mask but for once, William told himself smugly, it was the expression of defeat. He felt relaxed, released and triumphant. He reviewed all Rosemary's infidelities, her evasions and ambiguities and unexpected confessions, her games of cat and mouse with him when he had poked compulsively for the truth like someone exploring a bad tooth. He remembered his image of her eleven lovers in taxicabs, driving round and round Piccadilly Circus. He waited.

'Is it serious?'

He shrugged.

'How long have you been seeing her?'

'A while.'

'Are you in love with her?'

A yes-and-no movement of the head.

'All right – have you *made* love to her?'

'Uh-huh.'

'Tonight?'

'Uh-huh.'

'And before tonight?'

'Uh-huh.'

'Often?'

'Fairly often.'

Rosemary said, in a shamed voice: '*How* often?'

William knew how to play the game. His heart was filled almost to bursting with happy vindictiveness. He was hard put to keep a vicious smile off his face.

'When you say how often, do you mean how many occasions, or how many times tonight?'

'Both.'

'Well, which?'

It was difficult to see if Rosemary was genuinely sunk in misery or whether she was sanguinely accepting a switch in the charade that put William, for a change, in the role of tormentor. But it didn't matter.

'You'd better tell me how many times tonight, to begin with.'

It was William's moment, probably his first moment ever, and possibly his last. He chose a number at random and worked his face muscles until he had achieved a suitably solemn expression.

'Six.'

45

'I know this is the obvious corny question, but haven't we met before somewhere?'

'I don't think so,' said Poodle.

'Not at Mandy's Club?'

'No, I've never been there.'

'Or the Carousel?'

'No.'

'The Odd Box?'

'No.'

This was on the Piccadilly Line. Poodle was not very interested. He had thin lips and a slight squint and looked like a demonstrator in a Gas Board showroom or the manager of a small branch of the Co-op. She had noticed him once or twice among the few customers of her St James's cocktail bar, and had heard him use expressions such as 'your good lady' and 'would you care for something similar'.

'I know I've seen you somewhere. I have, haven't I, and you're not saying? Seen you somewhere?'

'You might have seen me in Polly's Bar,' murmured Poodle, to shut him up.

Her supplicant made a great sweeping gesture of snapping his fingers, at the same time creasing his face into a mock-excruciating expression of extreme self-mortification. Poodle, notching up two more cliches against him, disliked him even more.

'Of course! Isn't it amazing! Is – n't – it – *ama*zing! I must have seen you there a dozen times.'

'Not as many as that.'

'Half. I must have seen you half a dozen times in Polly's Bar. You know what it is, don't you? It's coming across someone out of thingy. Context. You see someone in a certain place and for ever after you always associate them with that certain place. Then when you're out of that place and you come across them somewhere else, you can't place them. Place place – you know what I mean.'

'Yes,' said Poodle politely, looking out of the train window.

'Don't you find that? You might let's say for instance know someone quite well, but always in one particular thingy. Environ. Environment. Then you come across them somewhere else and because they're not in that particular environment you can't remember them. You know you've seen them somewhere, but in this particular environ ...'

He showed every sign of repeating his observation in all its possible combinations but, the train having reached Piccadilly Circus, Poodle got up to go.

'You getting out here too? You're not wending your way to Polly's Bar now, by any remote chance?'

'No, I'm not,' said Poodle, who had decided to try her luck in the American bar of one of the tourist hotels.

'Or any other centre where liquid refreshment is traditionally imbibed?'

'It's very kind of you. I'm meeting someone.'

She thought that she had better take a short detour through Soho and shake him off. But he apparently had no intention of leaving her side. He was a little shorter than she was and had to trot somewhat to keep up with her. As they moved rapidly from street to street he kept up a running commentary on the various bars, pubs and clubs that they passed, giving a short description of each one and asking Poodle if she had been there.

'Now there's a very very interesting club, if you've never been in it. Where those people are going in now. It's a big resort with musicians, mainly, but the very interesting feature about it is you can get drinks at *under* pub prices. How does that appeal to you?'

Glancing carelessly across at the ill-lit doorway which he had indicated, Poodle saw that the two people just entering the club were her husband William and a large-mouthed girl who might have been an actress or a photographer's model.

'I'm not wild about musicians' places,' said Poodle after a longish pause. 'I think I'd rather go to one of those other clubs you pointed out.'

He lived in a bed-sitter in Paddington, at the top of four flights of stairs. Poodle was breathless and, after a dozen gin-and-tonics, rather dizzy. But she jumped quickly enough to her feet when he pulled the trunk from under his bed and opened it.

'Oh, no. Really not. I'm sorry. I couldn't do anything like that!' She gazed in alarm and bewilderment at the various collection of garments, instruments and equipment.

'Now wait a minute, Nina –' (She had given this as her name) '– Wait just a little minute. Give me a chance to explain.'

'No. Really. Honestly.'

'But you don't thingy. Comprehend. I don't want *you* to wear those things, I wouldn't insult you. I wouldn't ask you to do a thing like that. I'll be the one who's wearing them.'

'I couldn't. Truly.'

'You don't have to do anything, Nina. Just sit in the saddle and every so often you give me a little tap with the . . .'

'No. Honestly. I must go now. Really. Truly. Please. Would you unlock the door? *Please?* I *must* go at once.'

'All right, sweety, keep your voice down. If you don't want any part of it, you don't want any part of it. Game set and match. We've had a drink, we've had a giggle. If you want to go, you're a free agent. Nobody's going to murder you.'

'Thank you. I'm sorry.'

He accompanied her down the stairs. At the door of the building he said: 'No harm done, then? Goood,' and pressed three pound notes into her hand.

46

'I'm sorry to have dragged you round all those places,' said Jackie. 'I know you don't much like hanging about in clubs but the truth is I had a strong need of getting the weeniest bit pissed tonight.'

'Shall I open the wine?'

'Yes please, love.'

They were back in Marylebone Lane by now. Quicker than usual – for as a rule she liked to have a glass of wine and a cigarette at hand before beginning to talk – Jackie edged into one of her stories.

'Did I ever tell you about my Aunt Thelma?'

'I think so,' said William uneasily.

'About her going for the weekend to Paris, and she found a *pension* somewhere and dumped her case, then she went for a walk and couldn't find the pension again? Anywhere?'

'Yes. You did,' said William firmly. This was one of Jackie's marathon anecdotes, with many interior character scenes touching on Aunt Thelma's absentmindedness.

'And her passport was in the case, and all her money?'

'Yes.'

'And she went to the Embassy, and they told her to come back on Monday?'

'That's right.'

'Well,' said Jackie. 'I never told you the sequel, did I?'

'I think you did.'

'I'm sure I didn't.'

'I think you did but possibly you didn't,' said William, hoping that he would be able to stop her at the first milestone.

Jackie ran a relishing tongue over her red lips and began to recount the further adventures of Aunt Thelma, the meat of which was that she had gone on holiday to Majorca where substantially the same thing had happened as in Paris, with the difference that this time instead of going for a walk she had gone for a swim in the sea, and instead of sleeping on a bench at the Gare du Nord she had spent the night at the British Consulate in her Playtex bathing suit.

William, unable to recognize the story and force an end to it by getting a hundred points for total recollection, stopped listening. He had several things he wanted to think about: Poodle's holiday with Melisande and how he was going to pay for it; the habit of one of his neighbours in Tulip Street of throwing tea-leaves out on to the pavement from her front door; a spot inside his nostril. But gradually he became irritably aware that Jackie's narrative was forcing itself back into his consciousness. This was unusual. As a rule the sound of Jackie's voice was a background soporific, a subliminal luxury like fitted carpets or central heating. The talking registered on his ear-drums but normally he had the same resistance to the sense of the actual words used, if there was any sense, as a person living near an airport has to low-flying jets.

It was now as though a plane were coming in with one engine missing, and the ear was jolted to an alert by the variation from the familiar. There was something about the cadences and rhythms and stresses of Jackie's voice that jarred.

William began to pay attention again, catching her narrative at the point where Aunt Thelma was waddling happily down to the sea. Before long he had satisfied himself that the whole story was a fiction. This was unusual too. Jackie's discourses were always too inconsequential and pointless for them to be anything but true. It was not the improbability of anyone arriving in Majorca without having booked a hotel which struck him as odd, or the unlikelihood of Aunt Thelma being allowed to wander through the streets of Majorca in a bathing suit without being stopped by the police. Stranger things had happened to Jackie's numerous relatives. But her tale, in the telling, was altogether too neat. It had, what was most unusual, a beginning, a middle and an end, and there were none of the usual excursions or diversions or irrelevancies with which Jackie habitually padded her reports. She completed in seven minutes a story which, if she had been telling the truth, would have taken a good twenty-five.

'But darling, isn't it fantastic? You wouldn't think, would you, that the same crazy thing could happen twice, in the same year, to the *same person*? I mean even Aunt Thelma.'

'Quite.'

'I mean it *is* fantastic. Don't you think it's fantastic?'

He noticed that her voice was creeping up to the higher registers and that her hand shook slightly as she gulped back her third glass of wine. He felt enormously shrewd as he put his hand on her wrist and said:

'You want to tell me something, don't you, Jackie?'

'Yes,' said Jackie, 'I'm pregnant again.'

He didn't feel anything, except for a very obscure sense of elation. Fleetingly he imagined himself in a club bar such as the one they had been in tonight, saying to someone such as Pringle: 'You don't know when you're lucky, boy. I had it twice in six months.'

Jackie's wide mouth became a cavern of comic incredulity.

'It's so stupid, isn't it? I mean it's so ludicrous, darling. I've been terrified of telling you. It must sound like a tremendous try-on or something but I – am – bloody – pregnant.'

She sounded amused, the wry amusement of someone to whom misadventure comes so often that it has reached the point of absurdity.

William examined his reactions. As far as he could judge, he had genuinely become a cynic. He wished for the moment that he smoked, for it would have been fitting to have stubbed out a cigarette in a gesture of *c'est la vie*.

'Well,' he said, 'it's the hundred and fifty pound touch again, isn't it?'

'I'm terribly, terribly sorry.'

'It's pointless asking are you sure and so on, I suppose?'

'I'm ninety per cent sure. I haven't had the results of the tests yet but I'm ninety, call it ninety-nine point nine per cent sure. Vomiting, dizzy spells, the lot.'

William nodded. The surprisingly elevating effect of Jackie's news was wearing off quickly. He deducted the price of another abortion from his bank balance and saw himself handing over forty-nine pounds in notes to Poodle, assuring her that it was more than enough for a week's holiday, ten days even, in Brighton.

'How did it happen, do you think?'

'I don't know, darling. How *do* these things happen?'

'Well, before it was because we were both drunk.'

'This time you can probably put it down to my stupidity. I know what I'm supposed to do, but I'm never sure if I'm doing it properly.'

'H'm.'

'I really am sorry, love.'

He was now visualizing a bank account with nothing in it: unexpected bills, final notices, summonses, bailiffs, bankruptcy and disgrace.

'Look.' He found his voice dragging back. 'I don't want to ask you this, Jackie, and don't think in any case that I don't feel responsible, and even if –'

'You mean could it have been someone else?'

'Well . . . Yes.'

Jackie lowered her eyes and looked down at her silver fingernails in a way that reminded him of Rosemary. She tried to speak levelly but her voice, also, took on some of Rosemary's sullenness.

'I'm sorry you had to ask me that, William. When it happened the first time I thought it was so bloody marvellous that you didn't ask any questions. You just said, how much? And turned up with the money and that was that. You know? I wouldn't have minded you asking me then, because you didn't know me very well and I didn't know you very well and you would have had every right to ask. Although as it happens the answer would have been no. And it's still no, but I wish it hadn't been necessary to tell you.'

William, wanting to feel ashamed, was instead quite pleased

with the excellent character reference Jackie had given him. He was almost ready to drop the subject, but for the sake of his empty bank balance he decided to give it one more twist.

'What about all these people who ring you up?'

'You mean the rag trade lot?'

'Yes. I mean, I do believe you, Jackie, and if you say it was me then it was me. But they do take you out sometimes, don't they?'

'I've never pretended to be an innocent virgin, darling. I've slept with people if I've liked them, occasionally I've even slept with people because I've been smashed out of my head and for no other reason. But since you came along there hasn't been anyone. What do you think of that? I've been out with my friends, of course I have and you know I have. I don't want to stay cooped up in the flat all week and I don't see you very often, and if someone's a little businessman from Leeds or wherever he's only too pleased to be seen out with someone who's reasonably presentable. But I haven't slept with any of them, not for ages. And I can tell you, darling, it would have been far easier if I had – I've had long bloody rows about it sometimes. There's no reason why I shouldn't have done, come to think of it. I don't belong to you and I wouldn't have been doing any harm. But I haven't. I can't explain why I haven't, but I haven't.'

Large tears formed in Jackie's eyes. Made heavy by deposits of mascara they rolled quickly down her cheeks, leaving black rivulets.

'There's only been you, William. For months.'

The great mouth began to quiver. William took her in his arms and rocked her, comforting her in the way that he had comforted Melisande.

'It's all right. It's all right. It's all right.'

Jackie sniffled and gave him what with an ordinary mouth would have been a small smile.

'Am I becoming an expensive hobby?'

William smiled back ruefully. No reply seemed to be needed.

47

'I've been thinking about buying the *Encyclopaedia Britannica.*'

'Don't talk so bloody ridiculous,' said Poodle.

'On hire purchase, I mean. A thing like that's an investment and it would always be useful for Melisande – who is where, by the way?'

'In her room, sulking. You know she's turning into a thief, don't you?'

This came as a shock to William. Poodle had for so long kept off contentious subjects during their dinner-table conversation that it seemed like a breach of the rules. But she had been very subdued for the past twenty-four hours, and no doubt something was bothering her.

'If you're talking about what happened at the sweet-shop the other week I've already had it out with her,' said William, hoping this would help to bring the discussion to an end. The sweet-shop incident had been out of his mind for a good while and he did not particularly want it resuscitating now. At first he had worried about it, or rather about his own attitude, telling himself that if he was anything of a father he would storm into the sweet-shop and demand to know why his daughter had been accused and bullied. But this would lead to long, unpleasant arguments: witnesses would be called from the back room of the shop, the sweet-shop lady would talk about putting the whole matter in the hands of the police, there would be accusations and counter-accusations, it would be very messy, and he would probably finish up apologizing himself. He decided instead on a policy of boycott, and in a brief word with Melisande he had instructed her to buy her sweets in future from Woolworth's, just around the corner in the Fulham Road.

'She's been shoplifting in Woolworth's with Lil,' said Poodle.

'The baby-sitter?'

'What other Lil is there?'

'Poodle, I do wish you wouldn't let her go around with that girl. No wonder she's developing such a horrible cockney whine.'

'Didn't you hear what I said? I said they've been shoplifting.'

'Yes, well I don't believe that at all.'

'I don't care whether you believe it or not. One of those awful women across the street – Mrs Benson or Henson or whatever she's called – caught them at it. She saw Lil take a Mars bar from the sweet counter, she followed them round the store and then she saw Lil nudging Melisande and Melisande took a compact and slipped it into her blazer pocket.'

'She's taken this up with Lil's parents, has she?'

'Of course she hasn't. She wouldn't dare. Don't you remember when she complained about Lil using bad language, and Lil's mother threw a bucket of water over her? No, she put on her best pinny and waddled over to tell *me* all about it. I had a hell of a job keeping her on the doorstep – I expect she thought I was going to ask her in for a "nice cup of tea".'

'I imagine it was no more pleasant for her than it was for you,' retorted William. Sometimes he thought Poodle was a snob. If Tulip Street was not to become the fashionable outpost of Fulham the next best thing, surely, was to make the most of it and extract what one could of its plebian flavour. Personally he thought it would not be difficult to find something appealing in a visit from one of his working-class neighbours – it suggested the kind of polyglot camaraderie that one was supposed to get in Islington and Camden Town ('We respect them and I hope they respect us.').

'She was just being nosey,' said Poodle. 'And she was quite beside herself at the idea of the stuck-up family across the street having a kleptomaniac daughter.'

'And what about the compact? Did Melisande have a compact?'

Poodle took a plastic copy of an oyster-shell from her handbag and threw it with a clatter on to the table.

'She says she bought it, for me. She just goes on and on saying she bought it.'

'Perhaps she did.'

'She doesn't know the price of it and it wasn't in a bag.'

'And what does Lil have to say?'

'I haven't spoken to her. I thought you might. Couldn't you talk to her father or something?'

'Since I can never understand a word he's saying, and since Lil's bound to deny the whole episode anyway, I don't see any point in that. Let's just make a note in future that Lil keeps entirely out of the house. I told you she was a bad influence and this seems to prove it.'

'Then will you have a talk with Melisande and get to the bottom of it?'

'Yes, I will.'

They spoke no more for some time. William dwelt pleasantly on the theme of having a talk – a 'chat', rather, with Melisande. 'Now, chum, what's on your mind, eh? You know, we grown-ups aren't nearly as unsympathetic as you'd like to imagine . . .' But his stomach muscles tightened at the thought of what it would really be like, as he heard himself interrogating Melisande and saw her stupid, wooden expression.

Poodle's strange mood did not seem to have evaporated as a result of getting this business off her chest. Presently she said:

'As a matter of interest, where did you go last night?'

'Er – last night?' She had not asked him a question like this for several weeks and he was fractionally late with what should have been an automatic response. 'I was out, last night.'

'Yes, I know you were out. I suppose it'll save a lot of trouble if I tell you that I saw you. You were going into a club with a girl.'

The wife of a fellow dealer. A journalist, interviewing him for a feature about antiques in the *Evening Standard*. A collector, wanting to sell off the duplicates in her collection of porcelain cottages. An actress interested in buying prints. He plumped provisionally for the last – the only category, anyway, that Jackie could have remotely fitted.

'And naturally you want to know who she was and what it was all about?'

'No, as a matter of fact I don't,' said Poodle.

'Improbable though it may seem, she's a collector of –'

'I *don't* want to *know*, William. I just want to know how long you imagine we can go on like this.'

'– a collector of nineteenth-century domestic oils, I was going to say, a friend of a friend. How long do I imagine we can go on like what?'

'Oh, don't be stupid about it, William, you know what I mean. You're never at home, I'm never at home, we leave Melisande with a delinquent girl, neither of us gives a damn what the other thinks or does or says or.... All I'm asking is how long is it supposed to go *on*?'

'But what should I reply? A week? A year? What?'

'You're quite happy about the way our marriage has turned out?'

'I wouldn't say that but I don't see that there's very much we can do about it.'

'And you're content to drift on as we are doing at present?'

'Failing any other suggestions.'

'You *could* give up the shop and we *could* move out of this bloody street and take a flat somewhere and you *could* get a decent job where we'd meet people and go out and take some kind of interest in what's going on around us – but I suppose that doesn't appeal to you?'

'No, as a matter of fact it doesn't.'

'Well,' said Poodle. 'Next time you go into a club with a friend of a friend, don't be surprised if you see me sitting at the bar with the friend of one of *my* friends.'

'So in effect you're saying that you'll go your way and I'll go mine?' said William, trying to restrain his glee.

'I wasn't saying that,' said Poodle in a tired voice. 'But it's what it seems to come down to, isn't it?'

48

As far as he could work it out, he and Poodle now had the basis of an adult marriage. He thought she might have expressed her ultimatum a little more gracefully, but he was glad that their position was at last clear.

He visualized certain changes in his routine. When Jackie was out of her spot of trouble he must stop seeing her so often and begin to diversify his activities. He ought to have more friends, of both sexes: he would be at liberty now to ring them up at odd moments and suggest a drink or a meal or a drive down to London Airport for breakfast. He could start dropping more often into the Chelsea pubs and (when he could find someone to propose and second him) clubs. It would be refreshing to stroll round the corner for a vodka and tonic at six o'clock instead of going home, and to play the rest of the evening by ear while less fortunate husbands glanced at their watches ('You haven't got your wife trained, old boy. I come and go as I please.').

He drew two hundred pounds from the bank, this time earning a raised eyebrow from the cashier, for he had no more funds in his deposit account. A hundred and fifty was for Jackie, forty was for Poodle's holiday – she had decided that she and Melisande would have to settle for a couple of weeks at her aunt's in St Alban's – and ten pounds was for himself, a kind of incentive bonus to encourage the development of his new independence. It was lunchtime, and he thought that instead of having sandwiches in the shop as usual, he would go to a pub for a ham sandwich and some beer. He chose a large pub on the Fulham–Chelsea border, a place that was fashionable among models and young men in advertising. He had seen them sometimes on Sunday mornings, leaning on the bonnets of sports cars or perched on the low wall outside the saloon bar, drinking from pewter tankards.

In mid-week, he was disappointed to find, the pub seemed to be mainly the resort of bus conductors and commercial travellers. William sat in a corner under the framed cartoon of a famous writer who, although he had lived in Sardinia for the last two years, was still counted as the house celebrity. Furtively he began to count the fivers in his inside pocket, separating Poodle's and his own allowances from Jackie's.

'Well I'll be damned. I'd never have put *you* down as a lunchtime boozer,' said Pringle as he came out of the Gents'. 'But I'm glad *I*'ve run into you because I want to talk to you about *Mother*.'

'Whose mother?'

'The play, for Christ's sake. You remember *Voices*? *Lost* – are you with me?'

'I am now,' said William, essaying a joke. 'But I wish I hadn't been originally.'

'That's all under the bridge. It's got a new title now – *Call Me Mother Early Dear*. Bit gimmicky, but it's on the posters now so it's too late to change it. This is the situation. You know we set up a new production, don't you?'

'No.'

'Well, I'm telling you. New cast, new capital. I'd have rowed you in, as a former investor, but we wanted to do the whole thing on a shoestring. So we put it on at the Attic Theatre for about fourpence three-farthings, and as great good luck would have it Kleinsberg went in to see it.'

'Kleinsberg being . . .?'

'He's only the biggest bloody impresario in the West End, that's all. Well he likes it, he wants to put it on, and he's got a theatre. But.'

'But what?'

'The trouble is he's a bit skint at the present time and he's having bother getting investors because through no fault of his own he's had a few flops in the last few years. Briefly he's three thousand quid short and if we don't raise it for him we won't be able to open in the West End.'

'And what are you asking me to do?'

'I'm not asking you to do anything. But if you put in five hundred pounds you cannot repeat *cannot* help getting back what you lost in the original production. Plus a very handsome profit.'

William, after a short inner struggle, told himself that the best response to Pringle's brass-faced effrontery was to admire it. He could easily have felt angry and launched into a tirade about his financial plight, but this would have taxed him emotionally and he did not relish a bitter row with someone of such turbulent verbal prowess. Even at the prospect of giving Pringle a civil refusal he could feel his heart thumping. To give himself a little time he went to the bar and got a half pint of beer for himself and a large scotch for Pringle.

'Cheers.'

'Cheers,' said William, looking studiously into his glass.

'Well, what do you think?'

He took a deep breath. 'To be quite frank with you, and there's nothing personal in this, I think I've had about enough of theatrical investment for the time being.'

'I know how you feel but if you don't come in with us again you'll regret it. I don't have to come to you, I know scores of people who want to put money in, but I thought it was only fair as you were one of the original investors.'

'And *as* one of the original investors,' said William, gaining courage, 'I happen at this moment to be practically penniless.'

'Piss off,' said Pringle. 'I just saw you counting it. You must have about five hundred nicker in your inside-pocket.'

'Not quite as much as that,' said William. 'And it's ear-marked.' He now felt some need of justifying his position to Pringle. He also had an obscure desire to boast about the circumstances that had brought him to his present straits. Discretion struggled with pride. Finally he added: 'I've put someone in the family way.'

He drank some beer with a flourish. He expected Pringle to stare at him in incredulity, pity or admiration. Instead Pringle made a little tutting sound and rolled his eyes ceiling-wards, indicating that such a stupid admission was only what he would have expected of William.

'Jackie Douglas, or the other one?'

'I believe it's usual not to name names on these occasions.'

'It's Jackie Douglas,' said Pringle authoritatively. 'Well, all I can say is you're bloody green.'

The conversation was going the wrong way for William, who had imagined that by now Pringle would be bartering man-to-man confidences with him.

'Why?'

'It's your money,' said Pringle with a deprecatory laugh in his voice. 'You chuck it away if you want to.'

'But surely? What else can I do?'

Pringle made some play of silence. At length he sighed heavily, to suggest that he was having to make heavy weather only because of William's incredible naïveté.

'All right. *A*, how do you know it's you?'

'Because I asked her.'

'And she said yes, William, I'm sorry to say it is. What did you expect her to say – no, it might be the milkman? Jesus Christ, if I'd paid out to every bird who's come to me with that tale I'd be a millionaire in reverse.'

'And I,' said William with some pride, 'would be three hundred pounds richer.'

Pringle now favoured him with the incredulous stare he had hoped for earlier.

'She's not doing you for three hundred, is she?'

'A hundred and fifty.'

'Then where do you get three hundred from?'

Again William's desire to publicise his achievements got the better of his natural sense of discretion.

'It's the second time.'

'In how long?'

'Six months.'

Pringle repeated the studied silence. William was reminded of his maths master at school who, when he produced some foolish solution to a problem, would stare into space with an expression of patronizing tolerance getting the better of exasperation.

At length Pringle said, 'You know you're being taken for a ride, don't you?'

'I don't see why.'

'Twice in six bloody months? For a kick off it's well nigh physically impossible. For another thing, it's a very, very dodgy coincidence. For another thing you're not telling me that a bird with Jackie Douglas's experience slips up twice in six months. And for another thing I'm telling you, it just doesn't happen.'

All these thoughts had crossed William's mind. He kept his counsel.

'Who found the doctor – you or her?'

'She did.'

'Who made all the arrangements?'

'She did.'

'And you don't know the doctor's name?'

'No.'

'So all you do every time is hand over a hundred and fifty quid in notes? Then she comes back a couple of days later and says it's all right?'

'Yes.'

'*I* see.'

'Why do you say "I see" in that particular tone of voice?'

'Well, it's obvious, isn't it?'

'What is? What's obvious?'

'It's the oldest game in the book, mate, that's all. You've been taken.'

'But,' and William knew he was making only a token protest, 'Jackie wouldn't do a thing like that!'

'I can tell you things Jackie Douglas would do that'd make your hair curl. Blokes who've been through her and next morning she's conned them for a month's rent. Blokes who've bought her one bloody drink without shifting from the bar and she's been ringing them up for weeks after, telling them she's in shtuck. Blokes who've taken her back home with them for a quick shaft and she's round next day with a suitcase, trying to move in. That bird,' said Pringle with all the authority of experience impressed in his voice, 'will stop at nothing. But nothing.'

There was a long silence. Their glasses were empty and after a decent pause to give Pringle the opportunity of filling them, William ordered whisky for them both. He felt desolate, inadequate and ingenuous. He knocked back his drink and tried, unsuccessfully, to stare Pringle out. He asked:

'So what would you advise me to do?'

'Tell her to get stuffed. And if you want that loot in your inside pocket to work for you, let me have it.'

'No, I can't do that.'

'You're going to give it to Jackie Douglas? Then you might as well go in there,' – Pringle indicated the gentlemen's lavatory – 'throw it down the shithouse and pull the chain.'

49

After mature thought, he had no doubt left in his mind that Pringle was right. The only remaining dilemma was how he could best approach Jackie. He felt no resentment against her for tricking him: she belonged to a certain stratum of society and went by its rules and lived by its ethics. The fact of these ethics ought, on paper, to make his task easier: he ought to be able to ring up and say: 'Look, ducky, I've been thinking things over and you are pushing it a bit far, aren't you? You are being just that little bit naughty.' Which was what Pringle would have done in his place – but he was not Pringle and had never set himself up to be. On the other hand, he could not see himself, even on the telephone, handling the situation according to his own lights. 'I've thought the whole matter over very carefully and I really don't see how I can be expected to accept responsibility.' He had no experience of Jackie's temper, but he imagined she had one.

He was supposed to be meeting her on the following evening when, so she said, she would have got her pregnancy confirmed and made the preliminary arrangements for her second abortion. He could stall, of course, for she would have no need of his £150 immediately. Although if, as Pringle suggested, she wanted the money for some other purpose, she might press him for it and he would either have to hand it over or tax her with lying.

Clearly there was no point in chancing a personal confrontation. His only course was to write her a careful letter. He had a horror of 'putting it in writing' – one of his most miserable evenings with Rosemary had hinged on his refusal to write her a pornographic description of what he intended to do to her when they reached their journey's end weekend in Bristol – but there seemed to be no other course open. He need not sign the letter, and of course he would be very discreet in the wording of it.

My dear Jackie,

Unfortunately I have to go to a sale in the country tomorrow evening and shan't be able to be with you after all. It's rather an important sale of mainly tapestries and I have a French client who's especially asked me to keep a watching brief for her.

I'm sorry about this, particularly as I wanted to have a word with you about what we were discussing the other night. I've just been going over my bank statement and frankly it gave me a bit of a shock. The fact is that the way I'm situated at present I just don't see how I can raise the kind of money we were talking about.

I don't know quite what to suggest. You mentioned the other night that you weren't 100 per cent certain – so do you think there's a likelihood that you won't need the money after all? If you do need the money, is there possibly anyone else who might help? I was thinking that maybe some of your rich friends in the 'rag trade' might rally round!

Please don't think I am letting you down. If you really are in a fix I will do all that I can – but it honestly would be very difficult for me to get such an amount together at the present juncture.

The other thing I was going to mention was that things are getting rather difficult at home. I don't know whether anyone's been talking but I think I'm under a certain amount of suspicion at the moment. As you can imagine, this is making things rather unpleasant – particularly for my young daughter who is very sensitive to atmosphere and who is going through a rather difficult phase at present. She is only nine after all and I would hate to think that any action of mine might make her unhappy or disturbed.

What I am thinking is, would it matter to you terribly if we didn't see each other for a while? I honestly think it would be the best thing, certainly as far as my young daughter is concerned. If there is anything urgent you have to talk about you can always reach me at the shop. Otherwise I will assume everything is all right and will give you a ring when all this blows over.

Love,

W.

He read through the rough draft several times. He erased 'her' in the sentence relating to his fictitious French client and substituted 'him'. He crossed out 'at the shop' and wrote 'at work'. He deleted the signature, 'W'. He made a fair copy and destroyed the original. He read it through again and thought it quite a good letter.

50

It was possible that Jackie's initial reaction would be one of rage, and so despite the possible loss of trade he thought it tactical to stay away from the Bucket Shop for the day in case she telephoned and got him into an argument which could only cause both of them distress. He spent the morning at an auction in Kensington where he saw some Delft pottery being knocked down for two-thirds of the price he had paid for a similar collection. In the afternoon he tramped dismally up and down the Portobello Road, looking vainly for evidence that trade in general was slow.

He was tired when he got back to Fulham. It provoked his sense of the fitting to see Lil the baby-sitter skipping with a rope in the middle of Tulip Street, for all the world as if the GLC had designated it a slum-clearance play street.

'*Airza lidy bin uckina u.*'

'A lady?' said William sharply. 'What lady's been looking for me?'

'*A lidy.*'

'Did she call at the house?'

'*Naow. Jas gyve mea messinge.*'

'I see. And what message did she give you?'

'*Size few goa minny, she zinna Wi'i Baw.*'

'If I've got a minute, she's in the Wimpy Bar. All right, what time was this?'

'*Bar ar par.*'

About half-past. Half-past five, presumably. It was now six o'clock.

He asked in trepidation: 'Did she tell you her name?'

'*Size a tell you iss Rowsmri.*'

'Who?'

'*Rowsmri.*'

Initially he was too gratified to hear that it was not Jackie on the trail already for him to be able to feel angry with Rosemary. Then it occurred to him that Rosemary had evoked this kind of charitable response a damn sight too often. He experienced a quick surge of fury at her total lack of any sense of timing.

He said to Lil: 'If I give you a shilling, will you go back to the lady and say I'm very busy just now, but if it's genuinely urgent could she give you a message?'

'*I*?'

'Go and ask the lady if there's a message.'

He meandered up and down Tulip Street, feeling acutely depressed and put upon. A West Indian railway porter was coming home from work, a child clad only in a vest was urinating down the steps of the house that had belonged ephemerally to the colour-blind interior decorator. William's own house, with its ground-floor window-box now used as a communal ash-tray, was beginning to look to him as if it were awaiting demolition.

Poodle came out.

'Why are you hanging about in the street?'

'I'm waiting for Lil. She's running an errand for me to the picture-framer's down the road.'

'Have you had a word with her about that Woolworth's business?'

'No, but I will.'

'I'm just popping across to the launderette. Melisande's having her supper, and she wants you to help her with her French homework.'

He watched with anxiety as Poodle and Lil crossed paths at the end of the street. Lil was bearing aloft, like a flag of truce, what proved to be an incriminating message scrawled in ballpoint on a crumpled paper serviette.

Have left Robin. Had blazing row this morning – haven't been able to sleep since I saw you last. Keep thinking of you with this other girl. R. finally dragged it all out of me – he wants divorce. Am staying at Kensington Gate Hotel – been trying to get you all day. Please please please ring me or come and see me. Any time after seven this evening. I feel desolate. Please please please don't let me down now – I need you.

His anger at this latest piece of tomfoolery was tempered only by the fear of Rosemary's proximity. He had a hateful but panicky image of her sitting in the Wimpy Bar next door to Poodle's laundrette, stuffing herself with hamburgers and licking her thick fingers as she waited patiently for him like a spider making a welcome for a fly. His instinct was to screw her note up into a ball and stuff it down the grate, but the frustrating, infuriating, frightening thing was the five per cent chance that she might for once in her life have been telling the truth.

'Did the lady seem distraught?'

'*I?*'

'Did she seem upset? Was she looking sad, or biting her nails, or crying?'

'*Naow. Larfin.*'

'Laughing?'

'*Yair. Shwz torkina fella arra nex tyble an larfin.*'

He dismissed Rosemary and all her works from his mind.

'By the way, Lil. What can you tell me about you and Melisande going to Woolworth's the other day?'

Lil assumed a crafty, leering expression which Melisande had lately studied and refined for her own purposes.

'*Dow now.*'

'You don't know. All right. Did you take a Mars Bar from Woolworth's?'

'*Naow I din, I pyed frit.*'

'Very well, then, you paid for it. And what about Melisande? Did she take a compact?'

'*Laff tasker, woncher?*'

'Yes, I intend to ask her, Lil, but I'm asking you at the moment. Did Melisande buy the compact, or did she take it?'

'*She din tykey, she fahny.*'

'Where did she find it?'

'*Een Wooly's. Onna flower.*'

'On the floor in Woolworth's. All right.' But there was still a slight, nagging worry lodged in the back of his mind: 'And Lil – did the lady in the Wimpy Bar have a suitcase at all?'

'*Dow now.*'

'Or a large bag?'

'*Dow now. Down fink so.*'

'Here's half a crown for you. Take this note back to the lady, will you?'

He scrawled 'GO TO HELL' on the back of Rosemary's missive, handed it to Lil and went indoors.

51

'All right. *L'horloge de l'église sonne. Une heure, deux heures trois heures* ... What comes next?'

'Quarter *heures*, daddy.'

'Not quarter *heures*. *Quatre*.'

'Cat.'

'*Quatre*.'

'Cat.'

'*Quatre*, girl! Watch my lips! *Quatre! Quatre! Quatre!*'

'Cat.'

'You see, you don't try, Melisande, do you? You want me to do the work for you. *Quelle heure sonne l'horloge?*'

'*Quelle heure sonne*, er –'

'I don't want you to repeat it, chum! You're not a parrot. Daddy's asking you a question. *Quelle heure sonne l'horloge?*'

'I don't know, daddy.'

'*Je ne sais pas, papa*. You don't know what, the answer to the question, or what I'm saying?'

'What you're saying, daddy.'

'But you would know if you'd been taking any notice at all, wouldn't you? *Je ne sais pas, papa*. Do you know what that means?'

'No, daddy.'

'It means "I don't know, daddy." Now you say it.'

'"I don't know, daddy".'

'In *French*! For goodness sake! *Je suis une fille stupide, je ne fais pas l'attention aux mes lectures*. What does *that* mean?'

'I don't know, daddy.'

'Do you know anything, at all, in French? *Un, deux, trois* ...'

'But the whole point is, daddy, we only *have* French twice a week and I had *whooping* cough last term, and Mademoiselle Benchley won't *explain* anything to us, and ...'

'*Je suis une jeune fille stupide*. Say that.'

'*Je suis une jeune fille stupide*.'

'*Je ne fais pas l'attention aux mes lectures. Leçons,* rather. I do not pay attention to my lessons. Now we'll begin again, and this time sit up straight, stop fiddling with your hair and listen to what I'm saying to you. *L'horloge de l'église sonne*.'

This was his first real interview with Melisande since Poodle had told him about the shoplifting expedition. Jogged into action by his new words with Lil he had had the rather clever notion of broaching the subject in French. '*Aujour d'hui*,' he would say, '*ou nous sommes allees au Woolworth's, ou nous avons volé un Mars Bar et un compact. C'était très méchant de notre part*.' But before he had time to guide the conversation round to this, the telephone rang.

'Now here's an exercise for you, Melisande. See if you can answer the telephone in French.'

'I don't know how to, daddy.'

'Don't be so defeatist. *Trois, huit, cinq* ... You know your telephone number, don't you?'

'Yes daddy.'

William thrust the receiver into Melisande's reluctant hands.

'*Allo*. Er, *trois, huit*, er ...'

A woman's voice, very faint, said: 'Is William there?'

'Who-is-speaking-please?' said Melisande, as she had been taught to do. In the background, William groaned: '*S'il vous plait, qui parle?*'

The woman's voice said: 'Tell him his mistress wants to see him.' Then there was a click.

52

'I've told you, it was a joke.'

'A joke? It sounds like a joke. Who is she?'

'Why do I have to go on telling you? She's a journalist.'

'And she calls herself your mistress?'

'She doesn't call herself my mistress. It was a *joke*.'

'To a nine-year-old girl?'

'She probably thought it was you.'

'All I can say is that you have some very odd friends.'

This dialogue, or permutations on it, went on all evening. Sometimes Poodle began with: 'To a nine-year-old *girl*!' and then the musical-box conversation would follow its jerky course to: 'All I can say is that you have some very odd friends,' connecting with a creak to: 'I've told you, it was a joke,' and finishing on: 'She doesn't call herself my *mistress*. It was a *joke*.' Then, after picking up a magazine and throwing it down again, Poodle would wind herself up again and recommence with: 'All I can say is that you have some *very* odd friends,' and they would run through their roundelay up to: 'She probably thought it was *you*.'

At first there had been some sharp questions about Rosemary's identity, to which William replied that she was a high-spirited friend of Pringle's, a renowned practical joker who had once come to interview him for her magazine. 'Was it the girl I saw you going into that club with?' – 'No.' These passages were fined out of the dialogue quite early in the evening and they were left with the basic inquisition. 'And she *calls* herself your mistress?'

William's main fear was that the telephone would ring again. Immediately after the strange call he had left Melisande alone in the house (a mistake, because Poodle came back from the launderette in his absence, found their daughter sniffling, and got the whole story first-hand) while he went out to the public telephone box to try and reach Rosemary. He rang the Kensington Gate Hotel in a state of schizophrenic apprehension. If they had never heard of Rosemary it meant that her tale of leaving home was a pack of lies but that she was at large in London, in a semi-hysterical state, where he could not reach her and shut her up. If she had booked in at the hotel it meant that while she must have been telling the truth he would at least be able to talk to her and reason with her, although eventually he would have to face Poodle with the extremely ugly news that he was about to be named in a divorce. On the whole he thought he was not in any condition to worry about his long-term situation just now: his immediate and urgent object was to get hold of Rosemary and stop her making abusive telephone calls. It was with mixed feelings that he heard the hotel receptionist say that Rosemary was indeed a guest, but that she was not in her room at present.

Someone had once told him that it was possible to put one's telephone out of action by dialling the number from a call-box and then leaving the receiver off the hook. He had done this before returning home, but apparently someone must have been in the box and replaced the receiver, because his telephone was in working order again. So far it had rung three times, and once William had fallen over a chair in his hurry to answer it.

'And she *calls* herself your mistress?'

When the telephone rang for the fourth time – it was some tiresome washing-machine mechanic who kept arranging and re-arranging an appointment with Poodle – William's nerve snapped, and mumbling something about buying half a bottle of whisky he went out again to the phone box.

This time Rosemary was in.

'I want to know what the hell you mean by ringing my home and frightening my daughter.'

'Who's that speaking, please?'

'It's no use coming the innocent with me. It was a filthy trick, Rosemary. I know you've done some very peculiar things in your time but I didn't think even you would –'

'Yes, but William . . . It *is* William, isn't it?'

'You know damn well who it is.'

'You were the last person I expected to hear from, that's all I meant. I've been waiting all day to see you, you wouldn't come round to the Wimpy Bar, you sent that nasty message, you've let me sit here all evening, without ringing me –'

'I telephoned an hour ago, and you were out.'

'Then I must have been in the loo. But as for frightening your daughter – ringing your home – is that what you said? I truthfully don't know what you're talking about.'

'So it won't worry you unduly to hear that my wife is seriously thinking about going to the police?'

'If she goes to Scotland *Yard*. Don't you think I have enough problems of my own without creating fresh ones for you? I'm sitting by myself in a hotel room a yard square, Robin's thrown me out –'

'I thought you'd left him.'

'I have left him, but he told me to go.'

'So then you thought you'd come and inflict yourself on me.'

'But I wanted to *talk* to you, William. You've been telling me for the last year how important I am to you, how much we matter to each other. You can't just –'

'And then when for once I wouldn't let myself be imposed upon you ring up and abuse my family.'

'But I didn't, William. I swear I didn't.'

The telephone call took William through seven sixpences and at the end of it he came to the reluctant conclusion that Rosemary, in this respect at least, was innocent.

So then he rang Jackie, but she was out.

He went into the pub across the road, bought his half-bottle of whisky, asked if they could kindly give him the change in sixpences, and returned to the phone box.

Melisande had once given him a small address book as a Christmas present. For a long time it contained only the names of six or seven wholesale dealers with whom he did business, and the address of a fellow-officer in the RAF whom he had once met casually in the street. There were no other entries, for besides Jackie and Rosemary, whose numbers he dared not list even in code, he was not on telephoning terms with anyone else. One evening he grew very despondent about this and began to fill his address book with every number that might remotely be useful to him. He included Pringle, Trousers Primarily, the headmistress of Melisande's school, his barber, London Transport Enquiries, his insurance agent, the cable address of an American who had once strolled round the Bucket Shop and left his card in case William ever came across any authentic medieval swords, and several random tradesmen. Then, since the pages were still largely blank, he went through the telephone directory and entered the name and address and number of every club, night club and restaurant to which he had ever been with Jackie.

He now began to call these numbers and ask if Miss Jackie Douglas was on the premises. Most of the places had never heard of her; some went away to look for her and reported that she had been in and gone, or that she had not been in at all; others gave an abrupt 'NO' and hung up. The proprietor of Kemble's Club shrieked down the telephone: 'If she does come in she'll go out again, with my toe up her arse. She gave me a bouncing cheque last week.'

William dialled his own number, left the receiver off the hook, and went home.

53

At breakfast Poodle said: 'You know she rang again at four o'clock this morning, don't you?'

This came as a surprise to William, who had the conviction that he had been awake all night. He had certainly not been asleep when a church clock somewhere struck two, for at that hour he had got the idea into his head that Jackie, desperate at being let down, was on the verge of taking herself off for a ten-guinea backstreet abortion in Paddington. He had felt compelled to get up and go to his desk and look up the hiero-glyphical notes he had made from the *Encyclopaedia Britannica*. He saw Jackie sustaining partial paralysis resulting from tetanus of the womb, coming home a physical and mental wreck, and remaining his moral responsibility for life. But by four a.m. – at any rate it had seemed like four a.m. – he had convinced himself that she would not do anything stupid with-out getting in touch with him and giving him a chance to atone for his treachery. This reassurance left a vacancy in his mind which he filled with thoughts of Rosemary, of her impending divorce and of the wisdom or otherwise of going round to see her husband, throwing himself on Robin's mercy as the father of a sensitive nine-year-old girl and pleading to be kept out of it. There were eleven other shorn lambs to choose from at least, he could say, and the career of someone like Pringle, to name only one, could only be enhanced by the fashionable smirch of divorce, whereas the career of someone like himself, the father of a sensitive, highly-strung, defenceless nine-year-old ...

'I should think it was a wrong number, at that hour,' he said.

'It wasn't a wrong number, because I got up and answered it.'

'Oh.'

'Yes – "Oh!"'

'Well, I can only imagine that if it *was* this person who rang yesterday, she must have been very drunk to have rung again at that hour. I'll try to get some kind of message to her today and let her know that the whole thing is getting beyond a joke.'

'Don't you want to know what she said?'

'If she was drunk I don't see that it matters.'

'*You* say she was drunk, William. I don't know whether she was drunk, mad, drugged, hysterical or what. For all I know it's her normal way of carrying on. But what she said was, tell your fucking husband I want that money.'

William was nibbling a corner of toast. It seemed to him suddenly that he had crammed an entire slice in his mouth. He had to chomp rhythmically for a full thirty seconds and work his tongue to bring the saliva back before he could say:

'Then obviously she *had* been drinking.'

'So now she's a dipsomaniac? Rather than a practical joker?'

'Well obviously it *started* as a joke –'

'Yes, I see. A drunken joke. "Tell your fucking husband I –"'

'For God's sake, Poodle, be your age! It started as a joke, and then she had a few drinks, and then – I don't know, how the hell do you expect me to know? – I suppose it must have become some kind of obsession with her.'

'"Tell your fucking husband I want that money." What money?'

'Poodle, I have no idea *what money*.'

'Did you owe it to her, or have you offered to lend it to her, or is she blackmailing you, or what is it?'

142

'She was *drunk*, Poodle. It was four o'clock in the *morning* wasn't it? The whole thing started as a joke and she got drunk and how many times must I tell you, it became an –'

The telephone rang shrilly, seemingly having been re-tuned to a strident, fire-bell note of clamouring urgency. William spilt most of a cup of coffee in his lap.

'Yes?' He thought, wildly, of answering with 'Chiswick Laundry?' or something of that kind. It was useless, he supposed to imagine that the caller was Poodle's washing-machine mechanic, or a wrong number, or even Rosemary who would if God was merciful go along with a bluffing conversation.

'My name's Robin. I should think you've heard of me.'

He wished now that he had severed the telephone cord. He had thought of doing so last night and had spent some time prowling restlessly about with a pair of nail-scissors. Only the fear of possible electrocution had stopped him.

'Oh, yes. How are you, Robin?' he said with forced bonhomie for Poodle's benefit.

'I wouldn't say we were exactly on first-name terms, old man, would you? Let me come to the point – is my wife with you?'

'No, of course not. Why should – why should such a person be here?'

'All right, then, cock, let's not beat about the bush. Where is she?'

'I think I can tell you where the person you're looking for is staying.'

'Are you trying to be funny? I'm not talking about a person, I'm talking about my wife. Rosemary.'

William, wondering how long he could continue in this strain of ambiguity, was amazed in his panic to realize that he was dwelling uselessly on Robin's character insofar as it could be assessed from his voice. Rosemary had always given him a picture of a strong-willed, high-public-school character, relaxed but virile. What came over was the impression of someone with a slight Black Country accent who might have gone to a local grammar school. The voice, furthermore, was aggressively chummy – the sign of a weak personality. William felt pleased and superior. It was an effort to drag himself back to his serious predicament. He searched for fresh euphemisms.

'The person, the, er, friend, you're looking for, is to the best of my knowledge at . . .'

Poodle drained her coffee and, seemingly showing no interest in the conversation, left the room.

'. . . the Kensington Gate Hotel.'

'Have you spoken to her?' asked the Black Country accent.

'I rang Rosemary, at her request only. I had to tell her that my family have been caused great distress, and that my nine-year-old daughter in particular, should she get wind of this divorce business –'

'I'm not concerned with your problems, cock. The Kensington Gate Hotel?'

'Yes.'

Rosemary's husband rang off.

Going into the bedroom for his jacket, William automatically called Melisande to get out of bed.

'Let her sleep for an hour,' said Poodle. 'The train isn't until 11.30.'

She had two suitcases open on the bed and was packing her own and Melisande's things. William stared, taking in abstractedly the detail that for someone who never had enough housekeeping money Poodle seemed to have accumulated a vast number of dresses.

'What train? What are you doing? Where are you going?'

'I'm taking Melisande to St Albans today, William. I know she isn't supposed to finish school for another week yet but she's not very happy there and she's been off-colour lately and I don't see that it'll do her any harm to start her holiday early.'

'I see. This is the result of the mysterious phone calls.'

'You'll be far better off sorting out whatever you've got to sort out without us here to cramp your style.'

William considered this, and voted it an attractive and generous proposition. He folded one of Poodle's sweaters for her and put it in her suitcase.

'And when will you be back?'

'That's the question, isn't it, William?' said Poodle, giving all her attention to a square little arrangement of scent-bottles and tins of talcum powder in the corner of her suitcase. 'Whether there's any real point in us coming back?'

The house to himself. Finding Jackie, giving her the money, telling her he never wished to see her again, and then the house to himself. Not having to be afraid to answer the telephone. Not worrying about women writing to him. Getting a formal solicitor's letter off to Poodle to tell her about Rosemary's divorce. Possibly selling the house, and taking a flat over a shop in a more lucrative district. Being able to go out when and where he pleased. Not having to explain. Not getting that terrible knotted feeling in his stomach when he came across Melisande picking her nose.

He had to choose his words carefully, so as not to give Poodle a chance to go back on what she was suggesting. He rejected 'You're sure about this?' and 'Is this what you really want?' and 'Don't you think we ought to talk about it first?' and settled for:

'I suppose when you put it like that . . .'

'So you'd like us to go?'

'I wouldn't say "like". I don't see anything else for it, the way we've been going.'

'And this woman? This mistress? This joke? Where does she fit in?'

'She doesn't fit in at all, Poodle.' This was a mistake, for Poodle took it as a concessionary note and seemed to be wavering. He said firmly, not looking at her: 'But that's not the issue. I think that you're right and that it's better you should leave now.'

54

He was so drunk that he could hardly stand. He awoke to find himself leaning against the door – he must have fallen asleep while trying to let himself in. It wasn't morning yet. It couldn't even be very late at night, for he could hear the neighbours' TV at full blast – the 10.30 jazz programme on BBC-2, probably. But then the street lamps were switched off which meant that daylight must be approaching. Then it was a radio. It was the West Indian railway porter down the street, playing his radio.

He rummaged for his keys in his side pocket but found only a crumpled mess of what felt like used Kleenex. He must have a cold. He drew it out – a loose bundle of creased and crinkled ten-shilling notes, pound notes, a five-pound note, soaking wet and smelling of whisky. He felt in his top pocket. It was full of heavy milled coins, and a folded ten-shilling note wedged in the teeth of his comb. His trouser pockets, his hip pocket, his inside pocket – they were crammed with screwed-up, torn and soggy bank notes, and a vast number of half crowns and florins. Some of the money fell on the ground and he looked down at the litter of coins at his feet. He remembered now dropping the keys. He had been about to unlock the door when he dropped the keys and went to sleep for a moment. Or for an hour – he did not know.

He bent to pick up the fallen money. Half crowns spilled from his top pocket. Following the rolling course of one of them he saw his keys lying by a dustbin. Lil's parents must have taken to putting their dustbin out on the pavement. It added character to the neighbourhood if one was going for the Islington or Camden Town image, but on the other hand this kind of thing, like throwing tea-leaves out into the street and West Indians playing their radios, could only diminish the value of his property.

He picked the keys up and worked his way back along the brickwork to the unfamiliar threshold. It was unfamiliar because his door did not have a threshold. This was a blue door – his was lilac. He was at the wrong door. Was he at the door of Lil's parents. Or Jackie's, in Marylebone Lane? Neither, and he was certainly not in Tulip Street.

He straightened up, closed his eyes tightly and opened them again. It had the same effect as adjusting the framehold on a television set. A series of rapidly overlapping images settled until there was one image. He was in an alley of some kind. The music – it was not a radio at all – came from a basement jazz club opposite. So he was somewhere in the West End, and it could be late or early.

He looked along the alley and saw, remote but very clearly as if it were preserved under glass, a pool of vomit by a telephone box. He remembered now being very ill. A woman, a prostitute by the look of her, had come to use the telephone and had advised him to take himself off to the all-night chemist's or to the Gents' in Leicester Square. He was in the West End, and the alley was off Wardour Street. He had come out of the night club near Piccadilly with the hostess – no, without the hostess – and he had walked about for a while and been sick in a doorway in Coventry Street, then in the alley off Wardour Street.

Piecing together this evening little by little he forgot the immediate detail that he was not home in Tulip Street, and once again tried with his keys to open the blue door.

It had started in the morning, when Poodle and Melisande went off for the 11.30 train to St Albans.

He agreed with Poodle that Melisande should not know that this was anything in the way of a permanent departure – there was no point in upsetting her at present, and by learning gradually how things stood between her parents it was possible that she would accept the situation philosophically or at least without making a fuss about it.

The details of the separation were worked out in a series of brief conferences in the kitchen, in the hall, in the bedroom where Poodle was concluding her packing. For a short period, while Melisande was whining about some doll she wanted to take with her, they locked themselves in the bathroom and ran the taps so that she would not overhear them. He would pack up and send by rail the remainder of Poodle's belongings and such of Melisande's toys as she had not grown out of. The things they did not want would go to the Salvation Army. He would visit Melisande every alternate Sunday and take her for walks in St Albans, or when wet to the cinema, and on the other Sundays she would be put in a train and he would meet her at St Pancras. He would send Poodle a cheque every month. If he sold the house and moved into a flat they would split the profit, if there was a profit, fifty-fifty. There was no need to talk of divorce yet, but perhaps Poodle would see a solicitor and ask him about getting a legal separation.

There were other arrangements to be made but Melisande had started following them up and down the stairs, sensing that something was wrong between them. William gave her ten shillings, wished her a happy holiday, told her to be sure and send him a postcard, and – at Melisande's shrill insistence – kissed his wife good-bye. The moment the taxi drew out of Tulip Street he set off to find Jackie.

During the hall-kitchen-bedroom-bathroom negotiations he had given Poodle more money than he could actually spare – there had been a fraught moment when it had looked as if she would not go at all unless he gave her another twenty pounds – and now he had only a hundred and fifteen pounds left. He was sure that Jackie could find the odd thirty-five somewhere. He hoped that she was sleeping it off and supposed that he would find her depressed but no longer hysterical, and that she would not have had time to do anything foolish in the Paddington back-room area.

She did not answer the door. The curtains of her basement window were drawn but this did not signify that she was still in bed – often when he had met her after work and they had come back to the flat the curtains had still been drawn from morning. He walked round to Baker Street and located Mrs Wallace's cake shop which Jackie had once pointed out to him. There was a sign in the door: CLOSED FOR ANNUAL HOLIDAY. He went to a wine bar nearby where he and Jackie had sometimes been to buy a bottle of Chablis – he knew that she sometimes dropped in there for a lunchtime drink. But it was still early, the bar was nearly empty, and no one had seen her. He dialled her number from the post-office next door, and let it ring for a long time.

Doubtless if he went to the Bucket Shop he would hear from her soon enough but he did not want to be in the position of trying to break through a torrent of invective to point out that he had had a change of heart. He would rather seek Jackie out and put the money in her hand before she had a chance to draw breath. He took a cab to the West End, to look for her in earnest.

There was a Victorian pub in Maiden Lane called The Star

of India, where Jackie had often promised to take him. She had mentioned it to him as a place much used by actors because of its facilities for cashing cheques, and had several times referred to 'chums', as she called them, who went there. It was a slender start, but perhaps there would be someone there who knew her whereabouts.

The place was crowded, but taking a panoramic view in the caryatided mirrors William could not recognize any faces nor place anyone as obviously an actor. He bought himself a glass of beer and wedged himself into a corner next to a bunch of what he judged to be Irish road labourers. He would give it half an hour and then he would ring Jackie again, and go on ringing her through the day. Tonight he would drop into Kemble's Club and see if Pringle or any of her other acquaintances had come across her. These plans – 'dropping into' clubs, jostling his way to pub telephones to call his friends – appealed to him. He thought of Poodle and Melisande who about now would be just reaching the semi-detached home of Poodle's aunt in St Albans, all leaded windows and crazy paving. It was, William thought, just about their mark.

He listened idly to the road labourers next to him. One of them mentioned Brecht, another the name of a famous actress whom he was claiming, apparently from first-hand knowledge, to be a nymphomaniac. William studied the sturdy, Guinness-clutching figures in their workmen's duffel-coats and thick shirts. One or two faces were vaguely familiar, and he realized at last that although all of them looked as if they should be handling picks and shovels they must be, in fact, a crowd of Irish actors.

'Excuse me, do you happen to know Jackie Douglas?'

'I do.'

'And do you happen to have any idea where she might be at present?'

The burly Irishman whom William had addressed looked him up and down as if casting him for a bailiff.

'Who's speakin'?'

'I'm sorry. I don't quite . . .'

'Who wants her? Who are yez? *Fwat's y' naime?*'

William, with a sinking feeling that he had run across a

149

bulkier, Celtic version of Lil, said: 'Oh, I see. I'm a friend of hers. I've got some money for her and I gather she's rather anxious to have it.'

'Yez can bank on that.' The burly Irishman turned to his friends and inquired about Jackie. William was relieved to note that exposure to British television plays seemed to have given them some grasp of the Queen's English. One of them said, comprehensibly enough: 'She was pissed out of her tiny mind in the Corkscrew yesterday.'

This was a small drinking club to which William had been once or twice with Jackie. The burly one explained that the Corkscrew would not be open until the pubs closed for the afternoon, but that they would all be going there eventually and he was welcome to join them.

'That's very kind of you. Would you care for a drink?'

'I'll not say no to a draught Guinness.'

'And your friend?' William indicated the man who had volunteered the information about the Corkscrew Club.

'We're all on draught Guinness.'

For the next two hours William bought Guinness for the Irishmen and listened to their conversation. At first it was disappointing. Apart from another reference to Brecht (which brought a response of 'Fuck Brecht' from his burly companion) in the context of one of the Irishmen once having been to bed with a member of the Berliner Ensemble, most of the talk seemed to revolve on horse-racing, drink, poverty, and a pocket of fascism that seemed to exist in the Shepherd's Bush Labour Exchange. In deference to a generous host, however, the Irishmen after the third or fourth round began to exchange anecdotes about Brendan Behan. William, who was drinking more beer than he was used to at lunchtime, had the affable presentiment that he was on the verge of the kind of life he was looking for. He thought of Poodle again, and how out of place she would have been in such an atmosphere as this.

The Irishmen, some of whom were now singing mutinous songs against the English, bundled him to the Corkscrew Club, where they were joined by some raffish friends who also looked like workmen and who proved, in this case, to be so –

itinerant stage carpenters, scene-shifters and electricians. William, marvelling at the democracy of the stage, willingly accepted the chairmanship of a large drinking school. All his new friends had seen Jackie in one club or another yesterday; none of them had seen her today. The problem seemed to be growing less and less urgent as the day wore on. The actors had now switched to Irish whiskey, and William discovered that he could cultivate a taste for it too. His burly friend took him aside and in a voice gone hoarse with attempted diffidence said: 'I've not bought a round all the live-long day. Could yez not let me have the lend of a five?'

'Certainly,' beamed William, digging into his pocket.

He could remember going back to The Star of India at six-thirty and falling down the lavatory steps. He knew that he had had some more drinks with his Irish friends, but could not remember how he had got away from them. He seemed to remember lending the burly one another fiver, and then a cluster of hands reaching out for notes which he peeled off reluctantly like a bookmaker paying off his clients. He had the impression of running, or shambling, up Maiden Lane, to the accompaniment of Irish song which grew fainter. Then he was in a restaurant by himself, the same one where he had first taken Jackie to dinner. He could not remember eating anything but he could remember throwing up what seemed to have been a substantial meal afterwards. And then? What had he done then? Why was the pool of vomit outside the telephone box? Had he been ringing Jackie again? No, that had been earlier, much earlier. That was all settled.

With a great lightening of the heart William suddenly recalled that he had rung Jackie at about nine or ten or eleven o'clock, after an interval of four hours, and that a man had answered the telephone. He had total recall of, and for a moment enjoyed again in retrospect, the delicious sensation of release at putting two and two very quickly together and concluding that Jackie must have found sanctuary in the arms of one of her rich gown manufacturers. The man said: 'Hello? Who *is* this?' sharply, and he hung up.

His last recollection was of being in a night club – 'our'

night club as it would have once been with Jackie – where he had spent a lot of time sitting with a hostess over a bottle of champagne. She had seemed a happy girl and he had been very touched to learn that she was only putting on a brave face, for her father was gravely ill in Scotland and she could not afford the thirty pounds air fare to go and visit him.

He had dropped his keys again. He picked them up, together with a couple of stray pound notes and some loose change. Leaning against the blue door, William began to assemble all his crumpled banknotes. Straightened out, they did not seem to form the same kind of bulk. He checked each pocket several times. He had no more than forty pounds left out of a hundred and fifteen.

'You all right?'

A policeman, looking at him without much curiosity.

'Yeh. Morl ri', thang.'

'Don't hang about then.'

'Morl ri'.'

He made a great effort to stand upright and pull himself together. Wanting something to focus on to get his vision adjusted he fixed on the blue door. He recognized it at last as the entrance to Kemble's Club. He opened it, and staggered down the stairs.

55

Between the top and the bottom of the stairs of Kemble's Club he must have had a black-out of some kind. It seemed to have been several hours since he had opened the door. Perhaps he had been asleep again, and some sudden cry or shout had woken him up.

He now had the idea that it was New Year's Eve. It was so late – it felt late, and everyone was still drinking, in the fevered, dedicated mood of a special celebration. The club was even more packed than when he had been in it on the night of Pringle's non-existent party, and several people seemed to be wearing evening dress. There was a kind of soft carpet of noise, like starlings leaving a roof, and upon this were over-laid certain sharp, specific sounds: laughter, cries of incredulity or comic indignation, the scrape of matches on boxes, the crunch of glass underfoot, and someone shouting over and over again for morning papers. There was a sense of movement, but no one was moving, for there was no room: it stemmed, William could just see, from a swaying ballet of arms, a reel or Paul Jones for grasping fingers in which drinks were passed interminably from one outstretched hand to another.

'*Where* are the morning pissing *papers*?'

'Desmond's gone to Fleet Street. Hasn't Desmond gone to Fleet Street?'

'Surely to Christ they must be out by now. Papers! Morning papers!'

Then it had to be New Year's Eve. Late on, about three in the morning of January the First. Someone had given him a glass of champagne with whisky in it – or brandy? Where were the streamers? William closed and then opened his eyes: as if he had put on a pair of badly-prescribed spectacles that made some things clear while leaving others blurred he identified, across a swamp of dancing moon faces, the conspicuous figure of Pringle, standing by the bar in a frogged velvet dinner jacket with a silk cummerbund. He was holding a bottle of Dom Perignon with which he seemed to be conducting a chorus of rowdy acolytes, some in evening dress like himself, some in the over-casual garb of actors who are relaxing after work. 'Papers! Papers!'

'Here he is! Come on, Desmond, where've you been?'

It was New Year's Eve. A bearded figure in a dress suit, seemingly as drunk as William himself, fell down the last four stairs and scattered an enormous bale of morning papers over the people who were wedged by the banister. The eager hands, which a moment ago had been engaged in the quadrille of drink-passing, swooped like gulls and came up with flapping, smudging, crinkling first editions of *The Times*, the *Daily Mail*, the *Express*, the *Telegraph*. All the champagne glasses seemed to have vanished or to have been tossed aside to make way for the surge of newsprint. William half-registered a montage of distorted headlines skimming past his eyes: KENNEDY DEATH – NEW FACTS SHOCK; PRICES – TUC ACTS; TV MAN WAS DRUNK SAY POLICE: CAT GIRL FOUND DEAD.

'Where is it? Where is it?'

'There's nothing in this one.'

'Where is it? What page?'

Pringle's voice:

'We're rich! We're bleeding rich! We've done it!'

William could not see the connection. New Year's Eve. KENNEDY DEATH – NEW FACTS SHOCK. We're rich. He closed his eyes, to stop the room going round.

He heard someone say, far off: 'Bloody shame about Jackie.'

'Bloody shame.'

What did that mean? Jackie Kennedy? JACKIE KENNEDY – NEW FACTS SHOCK. And on New Year's Eve, too.

'LISTEN!' shouted Pringle. 'Quiet! QUIET! Everybody! Listen to this! *"In Call Me Mother Early Dear* Desmond Higgins, an author new to me, but who blah blah blah, has parcelled up compassion – listen to this: *compassion*, wit, humour and above all Jesus Christ Almighty *drama*; and rolled this *Jesus* compendium of talent like a mighty snowball into the valley of despond that is the West End piss-balling oh my Jesus *Theatre*. After the blah blah blah – *listen, will you?* – it is a relief to watch a play with guts, a play that not only has something to say but sings and oh Jesus *shouts* and dances it on the cottonpicking bastardising *rooftops*." We're rich! We – are – bleeding – *rich*!'

The noise took over, completely. The waving newspapers were only a physical extension of it. KENNEDY DEATH – NEW FACTS SHOCK, screamed the noisy headlines. NEW KENNEDY PROBE.

'Seen that Jackie's left us, Pringle?'

'It's not bloody surprising, is it?'

William found a disorganized bundle of newspapers in his hands. He swivelled over the headlines, from the news about Kennedy, or Jackie Kennedy, to the smaller items: PRICES – TUC ACTS and TV MAN WAS DRUNK SAY POLICE and CAT GIRL FOUND DEAD. There was nothing about New Year's Eve, or about Pringle being rich.

He was cold.

He had just sensed something, seen something or heard something that had given him a leaden moment of dead frightening sobriety. Something a moment ago. He tried to focus his mind, and in doing so he managed to focus his eyes. The page that had been dancing before him became intensely clear and intensely still, as though it were reproduced on microfilm and he was viewing it through a magnifying glass in a museum.

CAT GIRL FOUND DEAD

Actress Jacqueline Douglas (24) was found dead in her Marylebone Jane, London, flat last night. Police took away empty pill bottles and a note.

'Jackie' Douglas was known to viewers as the girl in a Tabby Cat Food commercial. Four years ago she appeared on Broadway in a revival of *The Student Prince*.

'The papers!' screeched Pringle. 'Who's got the other papers?'

Acres of them passed before William's eyes. Hands conveyed page after page to other hands: the members of Kemble's Club had assembled themselves into a human rotary press. CAT GIRL FOUND DEAD. ACTRESS IN DEATH DRAMA. WEST END ACTRESS DEATH RIDDLE.

He was aware that Pringle had somehow got across the room and was at his side.

'*We're rich!*' crowed Pringle, seizing William's arm. And then, realizing whom he was talking to: 'Or at least, some of us are. You,' he added, as an intense, malevolent rider, 'must be the biggest pratt since the year dot.'

56

It was the first time he had seen the house in Tulip Street with all the windows dark. Poodle, if she was in bed when he got home, always left the hall light on. It was so long since he had spent a night alone that he had forgotten he was afraid of the dark.

The dawn was coming up but the filtered light only sharpened the black contours of his home. Melisande's bedroom window contained the hard reflection of the sodium street lamp; his own was a clean, translucent, oblong. He thought he saw flitting shadows, the visual equivalent of the creaks he knew he would hear from every room if he went indoors. He decided to walk about until daylight, and in future to leave several lights switched on before going out in the evening. He did not in any case want to go to bed because the room would rock from side to side as soon as he closed his eyes, and even if he did get to sleep he would wake up with the confused notion that the rain was coming in or that a hot-water bottle had burst, realizing eventually that his pyjamas were soaked in sweat.

Supposing the police had found his letter to Jackie?

Very well, it wasn't signed and there was no identification. Supposing she had incriminated him in her suicide note? 'Police' – what was it? – 'took away empty pill bottles and a note.'

Supposing a post-mortem revealed that she was pregnant and the incriminating note tied up with the unsigned, unidentified letter. And would the post-mortem reveal that she had once had an illegal abortion? It would all link up. The unsigned letter, the man named in the suicide note and the illegal abortion. Then the search for Dr X, and after that the trial for being an accessory before the fact. Not to mention the inquest, and the scathing remarks of the coroner.

It was six in the morning and he was drinking coffee at an all-night stall in the King's Road when he stopped being able to edge out of his mind the simple, disturbing truth that he felt no grief at Jackie's death.

He tried to put this right. As soon as it was all over, as soon as he was in the clear, as soon as things were normal again, then he would have time for the luxury of sorrow. This was a firm promise to himself, and he would not be able to live with himself if he did not keep it.

But now? What about now?

He looked for something in his experience, some equivalent of his present feeling or non-feeling, preferably something of a comforting or sentimental nature that would give him warmth.

As a boy he had been given an old pocket watch by his father. It did not work, but by moving the hands about he could get the right time, pretending for short periods afterwards that his watch was only a little slow. He tried to mend it but knowing nothing about watches he could only fiddle about with the cogs and apply oil in various places. His father had told him that the mainspring was missing, but he did not realize that this was a vital omission.

The analogy struck him as appropriate, and he felt temporarily pleased with himself at his self-perception. It was daylight, there were people on the streets and he went home to make tea and have a restless sleep.

57

A brief report on the inquest appeared in the racing edition of one of the evening papers. Jacqueline Dougal, as she was described, had been depressed about her career, and she was also two quarters' rent in arrears. She had left a note to her mother explaining this, and had taken an overdose of sleeping pills. There was no mention of pregnancy. William remembered Pringle's catalogue of doubts on this score, and wished that he had been more unwavering in taking his advice.

Rosemary, after brief affairs with two Spanish waiters at her hotel and some other people, returned to her husband.

Poodle rang up from St Alban's to say that she would be coming home.

William, who had earlier decided never to look at another woman as long as he lived, adjusted the period of abstinence to six months. He would keep away from actresses and neurotics and find somebody reliable, possibly a widow or a divorcee with her own flat. He would confine his assignations in future to the daytime, to relieve him of the pressure of making excuses. He was also planning to buy some books on porcelain, and specialize in it.

Poodle came home without Melisande, who was staying in St Albans with the aunt for a while. Melisande had just celebrated her tenth birthday by appearing in the juvenile court on a charge of stealing an ashtray, valued at six shillings, from Gift Stores (Trading) Ltd. A hospital psychiatrist, a friend of Poodle's aunt, had given evidence for her, and she had got off with a warning. Poodle and William agreed that the police had made a great fuss over nothing, but that they were both culpable.

'We've really got to make an effort with that girl,' said William. 'We've got to get through to her somehow.'

'Yes.'

Both thought it necessary to make a statement.

'You know I had an affair with Pringle, don't you?' said Poodle.

William, despite the solemnity of the occasion, and the seriousness of the news about Melisande, felt an irrelevant, esoteric stirring of the blood. This – when everything was as it should be again – would be material for him. He did not know at present whether he should develop a morbid interest in Poodle's adventure, cross-questioning her until he had satisfied himself on every detail, or whether he should stifle his curiosity and preserve – or rather ferment – the incident for private, erotic speculation. But he could use it. It would be another change from feeling nothing.

'It was only a one-night thing and I don't suppose it evens the score but in any event I've come back. We did have something, William, though God knows what, and we might as well try to hang on to it. If you agree.'

'Well,' said William, wishing he could think of something more definitive, 'I certainly think we ought to give it a try.'

More about Penguins and Pelicans

Keith Waterhouse

Billy Liar

To Billy Fisher, Stradhoughton is one long subtopian cliché – from the garish neon sign, 'Come Dancing', outside the Roxy, to the St Botolph's wayside pulpit reading, 'It Is Better To Cry Over Spilt Milk Than To Try And Put It Back In The Bottle'. And the dimmer his surroundings, the keener is the edge on Billy's sardonic wit and the more fantastic are his compensatory day-dreams. Not surprisingly he lands up in trouble. For neither his family nor his undertaker employers take kindly to his fantasies; nor do his three girl-friends, at least two of whom he is engaged to! So Billy wades through a confused tragi-comic Saturday, as his past lies follow him here, there and everywhere. And at the end of it all, his bang of revolt peters out in an adolescent whimper.

Also available
Jubb

Not for sale in the U.S.A.